Tough Luck . . .

"Where do you think you're going?" Slocum called out.

Abernathy turned, narrowed his eyes, and fired twice. Slocum barely saw the other man's arm rise, but he sure as hell felt the lead whip past him. Guessing that the other man's impressive skills with a shooting iron hadn't been pure luck, Slocum glanced back to see if Abernathy had been aiming at something behind him. Sure enough, the younger Southard gnashed his teeth while struggling to bring his pistol up to bear. Any strength he had to complete the motion leaked out through the fresh hole that had been blasted into his chest. He let out a pained grunt, dropped his gun, and keeled over.

"What about me?" Slocum shouted.

"Fight's not with you, sir," Abernathy replied. "I suggest you count that as a stroke of good luck and be on your way."

DON'T MISS THESE
ALL-ACTION WESTERN SERIES
FROM THE BERKLEY PUBLISHING GROUP

THE GUNSMITH by J. R. Roberts

Clint Adams was a legend among lawmen, outlaws, and ladies. They called him . . . the Gunsmith.

LONGARM by Tabor Evans

The popular long-running series about Deputy U.S. Marshal Custis Long—his life, his loves, his fight for justice.

SLOCUM by Jake Logan

Today's longest-running action Western. John Slocum rides a deadly trail of hot blood and cold steel.

BUSHWHACKERS by B. J. Lanagan

An action-packed series by the creators of Longarm! The rousing adventures of the most brutal gang of cutthroats ever assembled—Quantrill's Raiders.

DIAMONDBACK by Guy Brewer

Dex Yancey is Diamondback, a Southern gentleman turned con man when his brother cheats him out of the family fortune. Ladies love him. Gamblers hate him. But nobody pulls one over on Dex . . .

WILDGUN by Jack Hanson

The blazing adventures of mountain man Will Barlow—from the creators of Longarm!

TEXAS TRACKER by Tom Calhoun

J.T. Law: the most relentless—and dangerous—manhunter in all Texas. Where sheriffs and posses fail, he's the best man to bring in the most vicious outlaws—for a price.

JAKE LOGAN

SLOCUM
AND THE
TRICK SHOT ARTIST

JOVE BOOKS, NEW YORK

THE BERKLEY PUBLISHING GROUP
Published by the Penguin Group
Penguin Group (USA) Inc.
375 Hudson Street, New York, New York 10014, USA

Penguin Group (Canada), 90 Eglinton Avenue East, Suite 700, Toronto, Ontario M4P 2Y3, Canada
(a division of Pearson Penguin Canada Inc.) • Penguin Books Ltd., 80 Strand, London WC2R 0RL,
England • Penguin Group Ireland, 25 St. Stephen's Green, Dublin 2, Ireland (a division of Penguin
Books Ltd.) • Penguin Group (Australia), 250 Camberwell Road, Camberwell, Victoria 3124, Australia
(a division of Pearson Australia Group Pty. Ltd.) • Penguin Books India Pvt. Ltd., 11 Community
Centre, Panchsheel Park, New Delhi—110 017, India • Penguin Group (NZ), 67 Apollo Drive,
Rosedale, Auckland 0632, New Zealand (a division of Pearson New Zealand Ltd.) • Penguin Books
(South Africa) (Pty.) Ltd., 24 Sturdee Avenue, Rosebank, Johannesburg 2196, South Africa

Penguin Books Ltd., Registered Offices: 80 Strand, London WC2R 0RL, England

This is a work of fiction. Names, characters, places, and incidents either are the product of the author's
imagination or are used fictitiously, and any resemblance to actual persons, living or dead, business
establishments, events, or locales is entirely coincidental.

SLOCUM AND THE TRICK SHOT ARTIST

A Jove Book / published by arrangement with the author

PUBLISHING HISTORY
Jove edition / August 2012

Copyright © 2012 by Penguin Group (USA) Inc.
Cover illustration by Sergio Giovine.

ISBN: 978-0-515-15104-6

JOVE®
Jove Books are published by The Berkley Publishing Group,
a division of Penguin Group (USA) Inc.,
375 Hudson Street, New York, New York 10014.
JOVE® is a registered trademark of Penguin Group (USA) Inc.
The "J" design is a trademark of Penguin Group (USA) Inc.

PRINTED IN THE UNITED STATES OF AMERICA

10 9 8 7 6 5 4 3 2 1

ALWAYS LEARNING   **PEARSON**

1

MONTANA TERRITORY

It never paid for a man to think about the end of his trail. For some men, however, the end was all too easy to see. For Rob Bensonn, that end was as plain as the long, wavy red hair that flowed past his shoulders like a greasy mane. He was a liar, a thief, and a heavy-handed brute. Those things had served him well enough when he'd entered the Montana Territory just over a year ago. He'd built up a name for himself and gotten plenty of folks to step aside when he walked through a town. In that time, he'd worked with other, more violent, men to forge something of a fearsome reputation.

When he'd strutted into the town of Tarnish Mills, Rob thought he could take his pick of damn near any woman and any horse that struck his fancy. His strategy for taking either was the same: by stomping up to them, grabbing hold of his prize, and knocking down any man who stood in his way. His biggest mistake was when he'd ambled up to the Split Log Hotel & Saloon and set his sights on the pale stallion tethered to the rail in front of the place. After going inside and having too much whiskey, he also got a look at a short blonde with a plump backside and breasts that practically spilled out of the front of her loosely laced blouse.

"Hey, darlin'," Rob slurred drunkenly. "I bet you been spendin' yer whole damn life in this shit hole waiting for a real man to come along."

The blonde's red skirts flared around her as she twirled to playfully put her back to him. Her white blouse rustled as she moved, the only piece of clothing covering the impressively rounded assets that had caught Rob's eye. "Don't presume to know what I think, cowboy."

Rob shoved away from the bar, which was about as long as he was tall. Following her between a few of the small square tables set up nearby, he reached out to grab her smooth, silky arm. "Cowboy? Ain't you know who I am?"

Turning to face him while slowly easing from his grip, she looked at Rob with light blue eyes and curved her red-painted lips into a smile. "You're too drunk to form your words, mister. Why don't you sit down before you fall down?"

"I'm Rob Bensonn." Since his proclamation wasn't followed by a clap of thunder or a gasp of fear, he craned his neck to look in either direction as he shouted, "*Rob Bensonn!* I killed more men than are sittin' here in this room!"

At the moment, there were only three men in the room. None of them were particularly impressed with the wild-eyed drunk.

But Rob smiled and nodded as if he'd caused the heavens to part. "I'm a good man to know, sweet thing," he said to the blonde. "I can take you out of this town and show you a thing or two."

"What makes you think I want to leave?" she asked.

He followed her through the saloon as she made her way to a staircase that leaned against one wall. "I know lots of things, darlin'. How about you let me show you?"

"I'm not interested."

"I got cash in hand," Rob said. With that same hand, he

rubbed his crotch. "And plenty more in my pockets for the takin'."

Having made it to the bottom of the stairs, the blonde turned to look over her shoulder. She gave him an enticing glimpse at the swell of her breasts as she said, "I'm not a whore." With that, she climbed the stairs and went to her room.

Rob was grinning as he turned to look at the other men in the saloon. So far, they'd been content to remain quietly out of his sights. Judging by the looks in their eyes, they either knew who Rob was or had pieced together enough in the last few minutes to be wary of him. He wiped his sweaty hands on the front of his shirt before placing one on the back of a chair and the other upon the butt of his holstered .44. "What's that filly's name?"

Two of the men shrugged before getting back to their card game.

The third man was a bony fellow standing behind the bar with sweat stains under both arms. He also shrugged and became preoccupied with rearranging some of the bottles on a shelf beneath a cracked mirror behind him.

Stomping up to the bar, Rob slapped a hand on the stained wooden surface. "What's her name?"

"Couldn't say for certain," the bartender replied. "Haven't seen her around much."

"That's bullshit!" Rob snarled. This time, he drew his .44 and slammed it down onto the bar. Trembling fingers curled around the pistol's grip and stroked the trigger as he pointed the barrel toward the lanky figure. "Tell me what I wanna know or I start shootin'!"

"Tess!" the bartender said. "Her name's Tess."

"Just Tess?"

"Far as I know. Now how about you take a drink and forget about her, mister? She ain't worth the trouble."

Robb's .44 scraped against the bar as he dragged it

toward the edge and then finally dropped it back into its holster. "Mister . . . what?"

Reluctantly, the bartender said, "Mr. Bensonn."

"You heard'a me, then?"

"Yessir."

"Then you know better than to make me pay for a drink."

"Yes sir," the bartender squeaked.

Rob took the glass that was set in front of him, brought it to his lips, and tipped his head back. Most of the free whiskey splashed down his throat while the rest dribbled down his chin and was soaked into his shirt along with everything else that had been spilled there throughout that balmy August. After pounding the empty glass onto the bar, he gazed around at that saloon like a tyrant surveying his newly won territory. "Tess, huh?"

"That's right, but take my advice . . ." He paused when Rob shifted angry eyes in his direction. Raising his hands to placate the drunk, he added, "*Friendly* advice. She ain't worth the trouble. She's—"

"She's about the tastiest thing I've seen since I got to town. Where you been hiding her?"

"This is the first time she's been here. She's just renting a room upstairs after being kicked out of the hotel across the street."

"What was she kicked out for?" Rob asked.

"I hear she was being too rowdy. She and—"

Once again, Rob cut the bartender short. "Too rowdy, huh? That's why she thinks she can stand toe to toe with me. She's a fiery little thing! I like my women with fire and I love 'em with big tits. That one there's got both qualities, so why the hell am I still down here?"

"Mr. Bensonn, I wouldn't."

The .44 emerged from Rob's holster in a flash. While his speed may not have been overly affected by his inebriated state, his aim plainly suffered. Even so, pointing the pistol a few inches to the left of the barkeep's face was enough to make the skinny man retreat until his backside bumped against the shelf of bottles.

"Gimme the key to her room," Rob demanded.

"I don't have it!"

Rob leaned against the bar so he could tap the barrel of the .44 against the other man's temple. "Where is it?"

"She's got it! It's her room!"

An ugly smile creased Rob's face, and a sour breath was expelled from his lungs in a chuckle that shook his entire torso. "She would have ta have it, wouldn't she? Guess I might as well go on up there and make her feel at home."

The bartender kept his back against the wall, where a short row of keys hung from hooks screwed into the same shelf bearing the weight of all those bottles. One of them was the skeleton key for every room upstairs, and if he hadn't been so full of whiskey, Rob might have thought to ask for it. Instead, he staggered toward the stairs and the barkeep glanced down at the shotgun he kept out of his customers' sight.

The barkeep wasn't a coward, but he also wasn't a gunman, and he surely wasn't anxious to face off with a known killer. Even if only half of the stories about Rob were true, that still put him miles above any of the loudmouths that the barkeep normally had to deal with. He left the shotgun where it lay, stuck the skeleton key in his pocket, and prayed that pretty blond lady had the good sense to know when it was time to duck out a window.

"Teeeeeesssy!" Rob hollered as he climbed the stairs. "Time for you to see what a real man's made of!"

At the top of the staircase, a row of doors were lined up along the wall to the left, and a banister on the right kept folks from toppling down to the saloon below. After grabbing the railing to keep himself from revisiting the saloon in the most painful and unconventional way, Rob shoved off and slammed a shoulder against the door closest to the top of the stairs. He bounced off, managed to stop himself before needing to grab the banister again, and came at the door with a vengeance. This time, he pounded his foot against it while shouting, "Open up, sweet thing!" His first kick shook the door in its frame, but wasn't enough to open it. When he tried again, Rob's heel sent it swinging inward to knock against the wall.

The room was just large enough to hold a modest bed, a wardrobe, and a narrow rectangular table with a washbasin and pitcher on it. The only person inside was an old man who was either dead or sleeping too soundly to be awakened by the commotion.

Rob grunted to himself and stomped inside. He grabbed the lower edge of the bed, lifted it an inch or so off the ground, and bent down to get a look beneath it. Only when the bed was dropped back to the floor did the old man on top of it move a muscle.

"What in flamin' hell?" the old man groaned.

Rob had already seen enough. He stormed out of the room and ignored the old man, who was still swearing at his back. By the time he set his sights on the next door in the row, the fog put into his head by the liquor he'd drunk was partly burned away. He kicked the second door in with one try and found Tess waiting for him on the other side.

She held her washbasin in both hands and flung it at the doorway the instant Rob stepped into her room.

"There's the fire I like so damn much," he said as the ceramic basin shattered against the doorframe. "Now how about a good look at them other two things I like about you?"

When Rob stormed inside, Tess made a desperate grab for the water pitcher resting atop the rectangular table in her room. There was just as much space in there as in the old man's room, which meant Rob was close enough to reach out for her in about two seconds. She swung the pitcher, but simply didn't have the muscle to do any damage as it thumped against his arm. Even if she'd had enough time or space to take a good backswing, the whiskey in Rob's system numbed him enough to erase any pain she may have inflicted.

"Get away from me!" she screamed.

Rob grabbed her by the hair and tossed her toward the bed. "You won't be sayin' that for long, darlin'. Not once you get a taste of what I got for ya." He unbuckled his pants one-handed and inched them down.

Before he could expose himself, Tess swung with both hands to punch or slap him anywhere she could. She even shifted her weight from one foot to another so she could kick him. He wrenched her head to one side in a jarring manner that made her stop what she was doing. Before she could assess if anything vital had been snapped, she was unceremoniously tossed onto the mattress.

Now that his pants were down, Rob's penis dangled between his legs, swinging back and forth behind the rumpled lower edge of his shirt. There was a commotion rising in the hallway behind him, but he ignored it in favor of groping Tess's breasts.

"Get away from me or I'll kick those balls up into your throat," she snarled.

The balls in question hung less than ten inches from the top of her boot. Rob lunged at her so quickly that she didn't have enough time to make good on her threat before he was lying on top of her and groping beneath her skirts. "You'll get your fill of everything I got before too long, Tessy, don't you worry."

Outside, heavy steps thumped against the stairs to shake the boards of the entire second floor.

The expression on Tess's face shifted from panicked to fearful in short order. When she felt Rob's hand slide between her thighs, rage took over. Her entire body stiffened and she pounded her fists against him. "Get off of me before you embarrass yourself! What do you think you're gonna do with that limp pecker anyway?"

He stopped what he was doing and propped himself up.

Rob shifted his weight, causing his penis to swing some more. Thanks to all the whiskey he'd poured down his throat, it wasn't much more than a wet noodle. He reached down to feel for himself. "You think that's funny?" he grunted.

She continued to struggle beneath him, but said nothing.

Taking his hand away from his privates, Rob made a clumsy grab for the hunting knife hanging at his side. His fingers closed around the handle and he pulled it free to raise it high. "What about this? You think this is funny, too?"

Tess looked up at him, too petrified to move.

Basking in his victory, Rob drove his blade down through the flimsy material of her blouse until the hilt pounded against her side.

She screamed, but couldn't twist away since the knife had pinned her to the mattress.

Those heavy steps from the hallway stopped at the door to her room and a voice roared, "Get *off* of her!"

Rob turned around to find John Slocum standing there like a demon from a bad dream. Dust was plastered to his face by sweat, which also made his shirt cling to him like a poorly crafted skin. For a moment, both men simply glared at each other. One was drunk from whiskey and the other was so enraged that he'd been reduced to something less than human.

Once that moment passed, Rob launched up from the bed and hit the floor while tugging his pants up over his hips.

Slocum stormed into the room, crossing it in less than three steps. He didn't take the time to check on Tess. Instead, Slocum lunged forward to grab Rob by the back of his collar and belt before the drunken son of a bitch could slip away.

"You know who I am?" Rob grunted as he was lifted off his feet and shoved toward the back of the room.

"I sure do," Slocum replied through gritted teeth. "You're the man that's about to see if he can fly."

With that, Slocum tossed Rob through the window amid the crack of splintering wood and the shattering of glass.

Downstairs, the barkeep winced at the sound of all the damage that was surely being done to those rooms. He glanced every so often at the shotgun that had yet to be moved from its spot and shook his head violently when the two remaining customers looked over at him with expectations written across their faces.

Upon hearing the shattering glass and thump of someone hitting the narrow balcony running along the upper floor, he breathed a little easier. The commotion was leaving the saloon. At least someone had the good sense to know when the hell to jump out a window.

2

"Are you all right, Tess?" Slocum asked as he hurried over to the bed, where she lay on her back. "Can you hear me?"

Her eyes had been closed, but now they opened amid the frantic flutter of eyelashes. "Yes, I'm—"

"Don't try to talk," Slocum cut in. He placed a hand upon her midsection to hold her in place. "And don't try to move. It doesn't look like you've lost a lot of blood just yet. That is, unless it's soaked into the mattress." He'd seen plenty of grievous wounds in his days. Sometimes it was better for an injured person to stay put so the pressure from their body against the ground or floor could hold them together. In order to get a firmer grasp on how badly Tess had been stabbed, he peeled back the sheets that had bunched up beneath her.

The knife was wedged in deep. As he pulled away the bedding, he eased her up a bit to get a look at how bad the wound truly was. What he saw beneath her didn't set right at all. "There's no blood," he said.

"There's a bit," she replied. "I can feel it."

Slocum took hold of the knife handle protruding from

her side. His intention had been to keep the blade in place so it didn't wiggle within a sensitive wound or saw the cut open farther with the wrong sort of motion. To his surprise, the knife moved freely with the slightest touch.

"Ow," she hissed. "That stings."

"Just stings?" Slocum mused. "Hold still. And I mean *still.*"

"I am holding still. Where's that bastard who did this to me?"

"I threw him out the window." Keeping one hand on the knife, Slocum placed his other upon her side. That's when he let out the breath that had been stuck in the back of his throat. "You're a lucky woman," he said while easing the blade up, "and that asshole was very drunk. Those are the only explanations for this."

As soon as the knife was raised up high enough for her to see it, Tess's first reaction was to twist around and feel the wound on her side. Slocum didn't stop her. She winced when her fingers touched the portion of her blouse that was wet with a small, spreading bloodstain. "I told you I was bleeding!" she cried.

"This knife was just snagged in your shirt," Slocum told her. "It must've nicked you on the way in. You know where to find a doctor?"

"Yes."

"Then find one. All you'll probably need is some stitches. I'd better go downstairs and scrape that asshole off the street before the law comes around asking questions."

"Better check the balcony first," she said while easing her blouse up to get a look at the shallow cuts along her ribs.

Slocum's face twisted into an angry mask. "God damn it! I didn't know there was a balcony!" He rushed over to the window, grabbed hold of the sill, and didn't so much as flinch when a small shard of broken glass sliced into his hand. "Shit," he snarled after catching sight of Rob hobbling down below to round the corner of the building. Not only had Slocum given him an unintentionally soft landing, but he'd also given Rob enough time to collect his senses and lower himself to the street.

As he hoisted himself through the window, Slocum grunted, "Drunk *and* lucky? We'll see about that." The balcony was just wide enough for someone to walk along the outside of the building. There was a railing that came up to about knee height before giving way to the sloping curve of a wooden awning. That railing had been busted directly outside Tess's window, and a trail of damaged or missing shingles marked the path that Rob had taken on his way down. Slocum stepped over the broken railing, squatted down, and slid along the awning to the edge. Once there, he grabbed on and swung his body over. When he let go of the awning, the drop to the street was less than two feet. He started running for the corner the instant his boots touched the dirt.

His horse was tethered to a rail at the front of the saloon. Upon rounding the corner, Slocum had to jump back to avoid being trampled by that same horse. Rob was in the saddle, whipping the horse's flank and pounding his heels against its sides.

"That's my horse!" Slocum shouted more out of surprise than in any genuine expectation of a response.

Like any loudmouthed idiot, Rob responded, "Not anymore!"

Slocum drew the Colt hanging at his side and sighted along its barrel. The pale stallion was a good horse, which was the only thing that kept him from firing. A wild shot could wound a fine animal, and there wasn't enough time to aim properly before Rob galloped away.

Cursing under his breath, Slocum looked around the corner for another horse. There hadn't been any others tied to the rail when he'd left his there and there weren't any now. And so, left without another alternative, he started running.

Rob turned right at the next corner, which would take him farther into town. While Slocum may not have been intimately familiar with Tarnish Mills, a dry goods store he'd just visited earlier was along that same path. He ran for it and had almost built up enough steam to charge straight through the door if it had been locked. Instead, it swung inward amid the tinkle of a bell set just above its frame.

"Hello again, Mr. Slocum," said the cheerful shop owner. He was a man in his late forties with a round face and eyes that were narrowed to a permanent squint. Stepping back to clear a path for the rampaging customer, he asked, "What's the hurry?"

Slocum came to a stop and looked around. "How do I get upstairs?"

"Ain't nothing up there but supplies for myself. I was about to get those things you purchased wrapped up and sent over to you. If you need them sooner, I could—"

"How do I get upstairs?" Slocum growled.

Perhaps it was a combination of his dramatic entrance and the gun in his hand, but the shop owner pointed toward a door at the back marked PRIVATE. "Right through there."

Slocum ran down the store's single aisle and almost knocked the next door off its hinges in his haste to get through it.

"Nothing's for sale up there!" the shopkeeper reminded him, but Slocum wasn't listening.

The store's second floor was nothing more than a large attic with meticulously formed rows of crates and stacks of papers. There was just enough space for Slocum to hurry all the way to the back and a single window. After sliding it open, Slocum took a quick look outside. "Of course," he snarled while pulling himself out, "this one doesn't have a balcony."

There would be time to curse his impetuousness later. Sometimes that quality paid off and other times it dropped him into even hotter water than where he'd begun.

Fortunately, the window was large enough for Slocum to ease through and lean outside so he could grab on to the lip of the roof that stuck out a few inches from the side of the store. With his heels perched on the windowsill, Slocum turned and faced the neighboring building, which was only a few feet away. There was a balcony on that building that was larger than the one on the saloon. Without giving himself enough time to calculate his odds of making the jump between buildings, Slocum pushed off.

He sailed for a second in empty air before clipping one boot against the top of the railing of the neighbor's balcony. His other boot landed on level wood as the railing snapped. It wasn't a clean landing, but allowed him to move on without breaking any bones. Slocum hurried along the side of the building, ignoring the movement behind the windows he passed and the voices calling out to him along the way. When he reached the end of that building, he set his sights on the next one. It was a single-story structure that looked sturdy enough, so Slocum placed a boot on the railing and made another jump.

Slocum sailed across, but fell short of a landing. His chest pounded against the side of the building and his arms flailed to find something to cling to. As he slid down, his fingers wrapped around a row of bricks that were set slightly higher than the ones in front of them. Probably intended to support a sign or some other future addition to the structure, Slocum used the narrow ledge to pull himself up and onto the roof. From then on, it was just a simple matter of running and jumping from one building to another.

The rest along the street either had balconies that Slocum could use or enough empty space upon their roofs to accommodate him. Slocum ran along the elevated pathway and jumped to the next building in line. When he heard the sound of a horse charging over packed dirt, he veered toward the other side of the rooftop he was currently using until he came to its edge.

On the street below, there was a gaggle of people and wagons clustered to watch Rob charge away. The fleeing outlaw had nearly caused two wagons to collide with each other and knocked someone down in his haste to keep moving. Slocum had made up some of the time he'd wasted back at the saloon and wasn't about to let any more slip away trying to deconstruct the scene below. All he knew was that he'd caught sight of his horse once again and had the means to cut Rob off before he got any farther.

Slocum used the awning of the building to climb back down to street level. Before anyone could ask what the hell he'd been doing up there in the first place, he raced across the street and cut down a narrow alley that wound a ways before opening to another street. Slocum hadn't been in town long enough to know all the shortcuts, but his sense of direction told him he was cutting a straighter line to the next intersection while Rob was forced to ride down the wider pathways.

His surroundings were a mush of sights and sounds on either side as Slocum raced to the end of the alley. He emerged from the narrow corridor seconds after Rob charged by. The outlaw made it about ten yards before Slocum's Colt barked once more to send a round hissing past his right ear. Rob hunkered down and snapped his reins.

Knowing he was lucky to have caught up this time, Slocum planted his feet and took proper aim. He didn't concern himself with the fact that he probably wouldn't get another chance without having to track Rob down the hard way. All he thought about was drawing a breath, steadying his hand, placing the sights where he wanted them, and slowly tightening his finger around the trigger.

The Colt bucked against his palm. In that instant, Slocum knew he wouldn't need to fire again. Rob was still thundering toward the corner as Slocum lowered his Colt to reload while walking down the street.

The pale stallion slowed a bit as it approached the corner.

When it made the turn, its rider wobbled in the saddle. Rob did his best to hang on, but slipped from the stallion's back and fell to the street. One foot remained partially wedged in a stirrup, and when the stallion felt tugging from that side, it slowed even more before coming to a stop.

As Slocum approached the corner, he could hear Rob's cursing above the rest of the commotion from the encroaching locals. He fit the last round into the cylinder, closed the Colt, and pointed it down at Rob. "Well now," he mused. "You've had one hell of a day."

"Do you . . . know who I *am*?" Rob snarled while pawing for the gun strapped into his holster.

Slocum had already answered that question and wasn't about to do so again. He'd wasted enough breath on this asshole, so he put an end to it with a swift kick to Rob's chin. The outlaw's entire body convulsed before going limp and hanging from one stirrup.

One of the braver locals stepped up to stand at Slocum's side. "Want me to fetch the sheriff?" he asked.

Pulling Rob's foot from the stirrup, Slocum took the stallion's reins and led it down the street. "Get whoever you want to clean up this mess. I want a drink."

3

By the time Slocum got back to the Split Log, a portly fellow with his shirtsleeves rolled up just past his elbows was walking down the stairs. Because of the small black leather bag the other man was carrying, Slocum asked, "Are you the doctor?"

"Yes sir, I am," the portly man replied. "Did you get hurt in this mess as well?"

"No. I wanted to make sure you tended to the woman upstairs."

"You mean the pretty blonde with the . . . cut?"

Knowing what parts of Tess's anatomy were truly on the doctor's mind, Slocum said, "That's her. Are you going for supplies?"

"No need for any of that. I'm already finished. Dressed the wound after cleaning it up. That's about all that needs to be done."

"No stitches?"

"I'll take another look in the morning. Right now, I think she should be fine as long as she doesn't strain herself. Now, unless you have a wound that needs my attention, I'll be on my way." If the doctor was wearing a hat, he would have tipped it. He had the same cordial, formal air about him as many business types or bankers.

Slocum rushed upstairs and didn't meet anyone else before getting to the second floor.

"You find the man who busted my balcony?" the barkeep shouted from the first floor.

Looking over the railing to the lower level, Slocum replied, "He won't be leaving town anytime soon."

"Mind telling me what happened?"

Just then, Tess opened her door. She still wore the same ripped white blouse, but it was rumpled after her struggle and from the doctor's examination. Many of the buttons were unfastened, giving him a generous view of creamy white cleavage. Large nipples brushed against the material as her breasts swayed freely beneath it. When she placed one hand upon the doorframe and leaned forward, her blouse opened a bit more. Large, sloping hips were cocked at an inviting angle, and the smile on her face grew the moment she saw who was outside her room.

"You want to know what happened?" Slocum shouted down to the bartender. "Find the sheriff." Then he turned toward the open door and walked inside.

Tess held her arms up and out to accept him as he approached her. Both hands locked behind Slocum's neck and her lips pressed against his mouth. It was all he could do to get the door shut before he was completely overwhelmed.

"So," he gasped when he got a chance to take a breath, "I guess you're feeling better?"

"That drunk wasn't even able to use what the Good Lord gave him. He sure as hell didn't know how to swing a knife."

"You should count your blessings. Plenty of drunkards have gutted people with blades a lot smaller than that one. Let me take a look for myself."

Tess started to protest, but quieted down as Slocum slid his hands along the sides of her body. He started at her hips, moved them up gently over her ribs, and drifted even farther until he cupped her generous bosom. She closed her eyes and smiled as he massaged her warm curves. "Ever since I hired you to escort me through this territory, I knew you'd be good with your hands."

"Is that why you waited almost a week before letting me near you?"

"Waiting for a good meal makes it taste even better when you eat it," she purred.

"We've been eating pretty well since we got to town," Slocum said. His thumbs teased her nipples briefly before he moved his hands back down again to unbutton her blouse. She squirmed as if to try and hasten the process of the buttons moving through their holes and sighed as the blouse opened fully to be peeled away.

Like any man, Slocum was drawn to her breasts. There was just something captivating about the large, perfectly rounded shape of them capped by the chocolate-colored skin of her nipples. He could almost feel them in his hands just by moving his eyes over the front of her body. With great effort, he shifted his gaze down to the spot where Rob had tried to stab her. Instead of the nasty gaping wound he'd been expecting when he'd first seen her lying on her bed with that knife sticking out of her, Slocum found only a pair of bloody scratch marks emerging from a patch of bandages held in place with a thinner strip of bandages wrapped around her torso. He peeled the dressing back to get a look. "That's not so bad," he said.

"Isn't that what I told you? I think you cut me deeper when you took the knife out than when it was going in."

"Aw, now I feel bad. Any way I can make it up to you?"

She smirked and slapped his hand away playfully. "You're being smart with me."

"Maybe a little." Slocum's demeanor shifted as he placed his hands on her hips and drew her in close. "Since you're doing so well, perhaps we can have us another meal?"

"You mean the same kind of meal that got us kicked out of that other hotel?"

"It's not my fault you can't keep your voice down in certain situations."

"On the contrary," she sighed. "I believe it is very much your fault. Yours and that sour-faced hotel owner."

"He was probably jealous of me." Slocum's hands wandered down to cup her buttocks, and when he pulled her hips against him, she was plenty eager to grind against the growing bulge in the front of his jeans. Their lips met and hers parted so she could slip her tongue into his mouth. Slocum's heart raced and his erection grew. As it strained against his jeans, Tess moaned in appreciation.

She eased away just enough to get a look at him while reaching down to loosen his belt. "Now that you've seen me safely to this town so I can get a look at my late uncle's property, there's a new matter of business to settle."

"What's that?" he asked.

"I need to repay you for tossing that sack of horse shit out my window."

"Speaking of which, we may want to get a new room. That window's still busted."

Her hands were busy and had already lowered his pants enough to reach between his legs and cup his stiffening manhood. "You really want me to wait?"

"At the very least, seeing as how this is such a fine and upstanding community, we should at least try to keep our voices down."

Taking that as the challenge it was, Tess smiled widely and lowered herself onto her knees in front of him. She lowered Slocum's pants the rest of the way down. His cock was stiff as a board when she finally wrapped her lips around it, and her tongue slid along the bottom of his shaft as she bobbed her head back and forth. She massaged his legs before reaching up to scratch at his stomach and midsection, sucking him hungrily, moaning as his erection grew to fill her mouth.

Slocum closed his eyes and placed his hands upon the back of her head. Sliding his fingers through her blond hair, he glanced back at the window to see that the light outside had faded to the dark purple of dusk. A shadow had fallen over that side of the building, but for all intents and purposes, the window was nothing more than a square hole in the wall. Not feeling particularly modest at the moment, Slocum shifted his attention back to the warm mouth gliding up and down his cock.

Tess placed her hands gently on either side of his rigid pole as she eased her lips all the way to the tip. Holding it in place, she flicked her tongue on him until Slocum's knees started to shake.

"What are you trying to do to me?" he gasped.

"Maybe you'll be the one to scream like a banshee for a change."

"We'll see about that." He didn't want to tell her how close she was to making him do that very thing, so Slocum gave her another few seconds to do what she was doing before reaching down to grab her arms and ease her to her feet.

"You want me to stop?" she asked in a tone that made it clear she knew the answer well enough.

Slocum didn't say a word. Instead, he turned her around and began stripping her out of her clothes. She wasn't wearing much to begin with, but he took his time in easing her skirts down over her hips and peeling her blouse the rest of the way off. Naked and breathing heavily with anticipation, Tess leaned back and reached over one shoulder to feel for Slocum. He was behind her, and when he allowed her probing hand to find his cheek, he pressed himself against her from behind while placing both hands upon her hips.

His cock was still plenty hard and it slid along the curves of her buttocks, all the way down to tease the wetness between her legs. Although he could feel the hot dampness there with a bit of shifting, he didn't have the proper angle to enter her. That sent a tense chill through his body, but drove Tess absolutely insane. A deep moan emanated from the back of her throat as she spread her legs and arched her back so she could feel him in the spot she so desperately wanted him to go. But Slocum remained on the edge of the Promised Land, teasing her with his thick member.

"You gonna make me beg for it, John?" she whispered.

"I don't know what you're talking about," he replied as his hands eased around the front of her body to cup her breasts. They were warm and heavy in his grasp. The longer he massaged them, the more Tess writhed against his body, grinding her hips as if he was already inside her. He gently pinched her nipples until she gasped and stiffened against his chest.

When Tess reached back and down, Slocum adjusted his footing to allow her to get one hand wrapped around his cock and start stroking. They stood that way for a while, savoring how each other's bodies felt. She explored every inch of his erection with one hand while Slocum used both of his to rub her breasts and eventually trace a path between them with his fingertips. Her nipples brushed against the palms of his hands, and Tess rested her head back against his shoulder.

Her skin was hot and sweaty. So far, she'd done a good job of keeping her voice down. In the hotel they'd stayed in the night before, she'd been so wild that the manager repeatedly pounded on their door, shouting for them to keep it down so the decent folks could sleep. Slocum grinned as he thought of that, knowing he might be sparking a similar commotion once his hand found the thatch of damp hair between her legs.

Surprisingly enough, Tess didn't cry out when he eased his fingers through her downy hair to rub the lips of her pussy. A tremble worked its way through her body, which Slocum felt as well. Her hand froze in place halfway along his cock as if she'd forgotten about everything else she'd been doing. Wrapping one arm around her chest to hold her in place, Slocum reached down with the other so he could ease one finger into her.

"Oh yes," she whispered.

After a bit of that, he moved his finger up along her moist lips to find the sensitive nub just above it. The moment he rubbed her there, Tess's muscles stiffened and she let out the beginnings of a primal moan. She stopped herself before crying out, even when her body trembled with the arrival of an orgasm. Once the little climax had eased up, she sighed, "Can't break me, John Slocum."

"I'm not through yet." With that, he grabbed her hips in both hands and moved her to the foot of the bed. Placing one hand on her back, he bent her over so he could fit his cock properly between her thighs. His movements were rough and urgent as he finally gave in to the impulses that had been raging from the moment this dance started.

Tess responded to every one of his unspoken commands, allowing herself to be positioned the way he wanted. Grabbing on to the thin metal posts of the bed's frame, she moved her legs apart to accept every inch of him. The moment his rigid penis parted the lips of her pussy, Tess closed her eyes and moaned gratefully.

It wasn't until he finally drove all the way into her that Slocum realized how badly he'd wanted her. Just looking at Tess was enough to make most men feel a stirring inside them. That feeling only became more powerful after Slocum had gotten his first taste of what she had to offer. No matter how many times he'd bedded her, Slocum still couldn't get enough.

Every muscle of her body moved in a way to make a man feel good. When he pounded his cock into her from behind, Tess gripped the bed frame and arched her back to give him something damn beautiful to look at. When he grabbed her hips tightly, she wriggled her bottom ever so slightly between his hands. When he fell into a steady, pumping rhythm, she tossed her golden hair back over her shoulders and grunted each time he impaled her.

Slocum reached around to place his fingers against the nub of her clitoris. As he entered her, he also pressed down on that sensitive spot and held his finger in place.

"Oh, that's not fair," she said.

"Why not? Don't you like it?"

"Yes, I . . ." She couldn't say anything else because he eased up on the pressure so he could rub her clit faster as he pounded into her with heightened urgency.

Tess gripped the bed frame harder and lowered her head as if she was bracing for a crash inside a runaway stagecoach. Her muscles tensed again. Sweat rolled along the smooth curve of her spine. Her breasts swayed in time to Slocum's thrusts. When he started pulling her toward him while pounding into her, it was almost too much for her to bear.

"That's it," he said. "You like that?"

"Yes," she grunted in a voice that was trembling with restraint. "Don't stop."

Until now, Slocum had been wrapped up in the game of trying to get her to make some noise. When he looked down to see the ample curve of her backside and her naked body rocking in time to his rhythm, he didn't give a damn about any games. Her flesh was warm to the touch and yielded to him naturally. Rather than try to get her to cry out, he listened to the stifled grunts and moans that she couldn't control. Soon those became more enticing than anything he'd ever heard.

She sighed when he entered her and grunted when she was filled with every inch of his stiff cock. Every now and then, words would escape her lips, telling him to keep fucking her and never stop. He glided between her damp thighs, pounding into her again and again. Slocum gripped her hair in one hand, tugging just enough to pull her head back while driving into her again.

Tess shook with another, more powerful climax, and it wasn't long before he joined her.

4

The next morning, Slocum awoke feeling more refreshed than he had in a long time. Part of that was because of a night spent with Tess, but another factor was all the fresh air that had drifted in through the room's broken window. Slocum pulled on his clothes and walked over to the window so he could take a look outside. Tarnish Mills wasn't much for scenery, but anyplace within the Montana Territory tended to be easy on the eyes.

The high country was only a few miles away, covered with a thick layer of trees and bushes. A trail, currently playing host to a single slow-moving wagon, snaked off to a distant river. All of that and so much more lay sprawled beneath a wide sky that made Slocum feel like an insignificant bump on the world. He nodded slowly while taking it all in. When he turned toward the bed, he got a nice view of Tess's naked body partially covered by rumpled sheets. That sight brought a smile to his face, but a knock on the door broke his train of thought before he could act on it.

As much as Slocum wanted to ignore the knocking, he decided to open the door if only to make it stop. When he saw who stood in the hallway, he reconsidered the choice he'd made.

"What do you want?" he asked.

The short man standing outside his room reminded Slocum of a giant bleached pumpkin. His body was round and his skin had the tint of someone who wasn't meant to spend any amount of time in the sun. A stubby neck was wide enough to make it and the head on top of it look like one solid stem protruding from the man's shoulders. "You need to see the sheriff," he said.

"Why? Are we being kicked out?"

"No, although I have every right to do so considering the trouble that woman of yours brought. I heard about her from the owner of the hotel across the way. This may be a saloon, Mr. Slocum, but it's not a brothel."

"I didn't pay for what I got last night," he said with a smile.

The stout man twisted his face into an ugly grimace. "You know what I'm talking about."

"No. I don't think I do."

"It's about that matter from yesterday. The one involving you and Mr. Bensonn."

"Who?"

"That gunman you tossed through my window. By the way," he added, "someone will have to pay for that and it won't be me."

Slocum had to blink a few times and look away from his strange little face just to clear his mind. "The sheriff wants to see me about that gunman? I did everything apart from gift wrap the son of a bitch and drop him on the law's front porch. What more does he want from me?"

"I don't know and I don't care. All I do know is that I was asked to deliver the message and it's proper for me to do so. Some of us," he stressed while shooting a glance into the room behind Slocum, "still know the meaning of the word *proper*. Good day to you, sir, and good day to . . . your lady

friend. If you want breakfast, it'll be served in half an hour."
Having said all of that, the pumpkin-shaped man spun
around on his heel and stormed back to his patch.

Slocum shut the door, snatched his gun belt off the floor,
and buckled it on. Tess remained still until she was shaken
by the sudden quake caused by Slocum's backside dropping
onto the edge of the mattress. She rolled onto her side to
face him, unmindful of the fact that the sheets had dropped
away to expose her naked body.

"What's all the fuss about?" she muttered while wiping
some of the sleep from her eyes.

"I need to see the sheriff," Slocum told her while he
pulled on his boots.

"Is it about you tossing that man through the
window?"

"I suppose."

She propped herself up and drew her hair back away from
her face. "Imagine that. What happened to the days when a
man could just dump someone out of a building and go about
his business?"

"All right, smart aleck. *You* deal with the saloon's owner
to see about fixing this window."

"Why me?"

"Because I have to see the sheriff. Apparently, my presence has been requested and it wouldn't be *proper* to be
late."

Tess giggled. "At least some of us still know the meaning of that word."

"So you did hear that?"

"Yes. I was pretending to be asleep so that little man
wouldn't ogle me any more than he already did when I paid
for the room."

"Next time a pretty woman asks me to ride with her
through the high country," Slocum said while placing his
hat upon his head, "I'll know to just keep on walking."

Tess reclined by arching her back and easing her hands

behind her head in a way that made her breasts stand out proudly. "Sure, John Slocum. You just try to do that."

Knowing when he'd lost an argument, Slocum left the room and stomped out of saloon without another word.

Although he hadn't had cause to visit the town law before, Slocum had passed the sheriff's office when he and Tess had arrived in town. He'd noticed the general state of disrepair of the place that day, but the window seemed filthier and the front of the office itself seemed dustier than he'd recalled. As he knocked on the door before entering, Slocum half expected to walk into a deserted room.

There were two desks inside the office, but only one of them had a man behind it. The other looked as if it hadn't been touched for several years. Stacks of papers, a few boxes, and some old plates were all covered in thick layers of dust. The desk that was occupied wasn't much cleaner. "Howdy," said a man in his late forties or early fifties. Although he seemed more than capable of getting up from his creaky chair to greet his visitor, he didn't make a move to do so. He wore frayed suspenders, a shirt that was either dirty white or light brown, and a bowler hat that could very well have been found at the bottom of a garbage pile.

Slocum approached the desk and asked, "Are you the sheriff?"

"Sheriff Roy Cass. That's me. What can I do for you?"

"I'm John Slocum. I was told you wanted to have a word with me."

Sheriff Cass considered that for a few seconds. His jaw shifted back and forth, and his face scrunched up as if he was focusing heavily on the cud he was chewing. After a few seconds, his eyebrows snapped to attention and he said, "That's right! The fellow who tossed that man through a window!"

"Yes," Slocum replied while taking a look around. There were a few doors at the back of the room, but neither of them seemed sturdy enough for a jail. "Where is he, by the way?"

"Cooling his heels in the smokehouse out back," Cass said with a lopsided grin. "It's what passes for a jail around here. Does the job well enough and smells like Christmas supper."

"Sounds delightful. What do you want from me?"

For a moment, the lawman looked as though he didn't know what Slocum was talking about. Then he snapped his fingers and reached into one of his desk drawers. "Oh, that! Frankly, I'm surprised you didn't come to me on your own. Hope you didn't think it was anything sinister."

"Normally being summoned by a lawman either means you're in trouble or you'll be asked to do something. I'm not really in the mood for either."

"How about cash?" the sheriff asked as he set a small metal box onto his desk, opened it, and started counting out bills.

Slocum wasn't desperate for money, but he knew all too well that the winds of fortune could blow him off course at any given moment. It was never wise to turn down money when it was handed over unless there were too many strings attached. Unfortunately, there were always strings. When the stack of money was placed in front of him, Slocum asked, "What's that for?"

"The bounty on Rob Bensonn's hide. You delivered him to me wrapped up nice and neat, so it's all yours."

"I'm not a bounty hunter."

"Then perhaps you should consider it as a profession because you did a hell of a job."

Slocum picked up the money and counted it. There were three hundred and fifty dollars in the stack. "So you know who Rob Bensonn is?"

"Sure I do. He can't go five damn minutes without reminding everyone about it."

"And you knew he was in town?"

"It's my town," the lawman replied. "I know most everything that goes on here."

"If it's your town, then why the hell weren't you protecting it?"

Sheriff Cass placed both hands flat upon his desk and rose up from his chair. It took quite a bit of effort and he wheezed slightly when he said, "Pardon me?"

"I think you heard me just fine, Sheriff. This is your town and there's a killer walking your streets, bragging about all the blood he's spilled to anyone who'll listen."

"Most of that kind of talk is just that. Talk. The men who do the talking ain't usually nothing more than liars or drunks."

Slocum felt his fists start to clench. "Maybe you should ask the woman who was nearly raped . . . or worse . . . how that animal was full of nothing but talk."

"That animal is in a cage where he belongs. Thanks to you. If you want to insult me, I'll ask you kindly to leave my office before I toss you out on your ear. If you want to take your money, you can do it and enjoy the rest of your stay in Tarnish Mills. I'd suggest you do the latter, sir."

"Could you answer me two questions?"

"What are your questions?"

"How long has Rob Bensonn been in town?"

The sheriff shrugged. "Couldn't say for certain. A few days, maybe."

"And how much is your salary for a few days?"

"Why do you need to know that?"

"The way I see it," Slocum replied, "that's all money I should get since it was me doing your damn job for you in that stretch of time."

As the lawman's eyes narrowed into angry slits, he leaned forward with enough force to make his desk creak beneath his hands. "Take your money and get the hell out of my office."

"Gladly," Slocum grunted. He stuffed the cash into his pocket and left.

5

A few hours later, Slocum had had a big breakfast, drunk his fill of some freshly brewed coffee, and was lying on his bed with Tess riding him like he was a bucking bronco. The window was still broken, but the curtains were drawn and billowing with a warm breeze that came in from the west. Tess was naked as a jaybird, pressing her hands flat against his chest and bouncing on his rigid cock in a way that made her breasts move with a rhythm of their own. They were still locked in a battle of wills to see who could go the longest without making a noise, so she chewed on the inside of one cheek as she took every inch of Slocum's erection deep inside her.

He let out a breath and reached up with both hands to cup her tits. Slocum never tired of how they felt in his grasp. When he teased her nipples the way she liked so much, Tess sucked in a sharp breath and let it out in a wavering sigh. That sound was music to his ears. Before she was finished, her sigh was lost amid the cracking of gunfire.

"What was that?" she asked as she came to a sudden stop.

"Who cares? Just keep going."

Tess shifted her weight, which didn't feel bad from Slocum's angle. Rather than pick up where she'd left off, she strained to lean toward the window. "I think those were gunshots."

He knew they were shots, but Slocum would be damned if he was going to be the one to push her away so he could walk toward that window. "Could've been anything. Don't worry about it." When Tess didn't resume her rocking motions, Slocum grabbed her hips and started pumping up into her.

She shook her head at first while squirming in his grasp. After a few powerful thrusts, she clenched her eyes shut and stayed put. "Right there," she whispered while doing her best to maintain the strange posture she'd taken to get a better look at the window.

Slocum smiled, knowing he was back in business. Keeping one hand on her hip, he slid the other one up over her stomach and to the narrow valley between her swaying breasts. He pumped into her again. Moaning, Tess ground her hips in a way that made him feel—

"Good Lord!" she said as another volley of shots rolled through the air.

Before Slocum could set her mind at ease again, people outside started yelling back and forth about a gunfight in the street.

When he looked up at Tess, she was too distracted by the window to notice much of anything else. Every part of her body that could lean toward that side of the room was doing so. He could even feel the muscles in her legs and thighs tensing to carry her up and off the bed. "God damn it," he growled. "Go on and have a look!"

She climbed down and grabbed the first thing she could use to cover herself before pulling the curtains aside. Holding a blanket against the front of her body, she looked down and mused, "There's a whole lot of riled-up folks down there."

"I think I'm going to take my horse out for a ride."

"What?" she asked while reeling around to face him.

Slocum shrugged his shoulders and scooped up his clothes. "I'm sure he'd like a chance to stretch his legs. So would I."

"John! It sounds like someone was hurt."

"Then maybe someone should fetch the sheriff."

Tess didn't say anything to that. She didn't need to do much more than glare sternly at him for some of the quietest moments they'd shared since their paths had crossed. Unable and unwilling to weather much more of that storm, Slocum grabbed his gun belt and cinched it around his waist. "Fine. If that's what you want, I'll go marching out in the middle of all that confusion and see about creating some more. Happy?"

Her sternness melted away to be replaced by a warm smile. "You're a good man, John Slocum."

"And why do good men always get the short end of the stick?"

"I treat good men pretty well. When you come back," she added while sidling up to him and allowing the blanket to fall away from her body, "I'll show you firsthand."

Then Tess planted a kiss on Slocum that would linger with him for years to come. In quiet moments when he had nothing to do besides reflect on some of his finer days, in difficult moments when he needed something good to cling to, in moments when his mind was blank and ready for a surprise memory to sneak up on him, he would feel that kiss once again.

Her tongue eased across his lips, and her mouth pressed long and hard against his. Their hands wandered, and when she finally stepped back, Slocum wasn't able to catch his breath right away. Not that he was about to let her know all that. Slocum nodded and turned as if he was simply leaving one room and heading into another.

If he was forced to place a wager at that moment, Slocum

would have bet every dollar he'd been given that she was staring at him with a wide, pretty, and exceedingly victorious smile on her face.

The saloon had been so quiet that his footsteps echoed through the place. The large window bearing the Split Log's name was alive with a performance of shadows racing across the other side of the glass. Voices, although muffled, were loud enough for him to make out panicked words and shouts.

Pausing at the front door, he turned toward the bartender and asked, "What the hell is going on?"

"Sounds like someone's shooting."

Instead of staying put to get more useless answers from the barkeep, Slocum went outside and allowed himself to be swept into the flow of people moving down the street. It wasn't exactly a stampede, but there were enough people to form a current that brought Slocum to a spot in the street within spitting distance of the sheriff's office.

The front door of the office was wide open. Since no fewer than ten locals were clustered around the entrance, Slocum couldn't see much. When a strong breeze got the door to swing, it knocked against something and came to an abrupt stop.

"Will everyone please stand back?" The man who'd just spoken rose up from the crowd with his arms held high above his head. He was the doctor who'd tended to Tess's cuts. Although he wasn't a particularly tall man, he seemed like a giant since everyone around him was hunched over to look at whatever had kept the door from shutting.

Slocum shoved through the crowd all the way to the front to find Sheriff Cass lying flat on his back with his legs splayed out in front of him. Before his door could knock him in the shoulder again, the doctor braced his foot against it. "What happened here?" Slocum asked.

The doctor didn't look up from his patient. The sheriff's shirt was soaked through with blood. He pulled it open to reveal a large, sucking chest wound. "Step back and give me room to work!" the doctor commanded.

Like all the others who'd been standing there, Slocum couldn't take his eyes off the chest wound. It was a small pool that looked too dark to be blood. Small bubbles rose every now and then as the lawman's life drained out for anyone to see. Slocum averted his eyes while thinking about the last time he'd spoken with Sheriff Cass. The pangs of guilt he felt became worse when he saw the thick peg of chipped wood where the sheriff's left leg beneath the knee should have been. So that's why he hadn't strayed from his desk when Slocum had been there before.

"Jesus Christ," Slocum sighed, feeling like the biggest ass in the territory.

"If you're going to blaspheme, do it somewhere else," the doctor said. "This man needs all the help he can get no matter where it comes from."

"Tell me what happened," Slocum demanded.

"I just got here and this is how I found him. Now step aside!"

Slocum put his back to the lawman and reflexively struck a defensive posture when he saw how many other people were trying to get a closer look. Lowering his head like a dog with its hackles raised, he snarled, "Someone tell me what happened!"

"The sheriff was stepping outside when somebody called him out."

Having narrowed the location of the speaker down to one section of the crowd, Slocum shifted his eyes in that direction and asked, "Who called him out?"

A young man still in his late teens stared at him with wide eyes. "He was some old-timer. He told the sheriff to cut Rob Bensonn loose or else he'd send him straight to hell. Send the sheriff, I mean."

"Was the old man a friend of Bensonn's?"

"I don't know that, but I guess the old man is a killer. I heard Rob Bensonn is—"

"Yeah," Slocum snapped. "I've already heard plenty about Bensonn. I want to hear about the old man."

Since the doctor had recruited one other man to drag the sheriff inside and close the door, the rest of the crowd was left without a show to watch. One of the others who spoke up looked to be older than the kid in his teens, but not by much. "That old man was a damned killer if I ever saw one. Looked tougher than leather and drew his gun faster than I ever seen."

"He told the sheriff to cut Rob loose," Slocum recited. "And when he didn't, the old man gunned him down?"

Almost everyone in the crowd nodded. "I swear I ain't never seen someone shoot that fast before," the older teen said. "The sheriff didn't even get a chance to touch his pistol."

"That's not speed," Slocum said. "That's firing when the man in front of you isn't looking or wasn't ready."

"He was ready," the younger of the two spokesmen replied. "Sheriff Cass said he aimed to kill anyone who took another step toward that smokehouse. The old man shouted for him to toss his keys and the sheriff told him to go to hell. Next thing I know, the old man put a bullet into the sheriff!"

"That's right," a grizzled man with a head of gray hair said through a mouthful of tobacco. "Quicker than a hiccup."

"It sure was that fast!" the younger man said. After that, lots of others from the crowd chimed in with their accounts of just how quickly the killer had moved when he'd put the sheriff down. Some of the eyewitnesses claimed they hadn't even seen the old man's arm move at all apart from a blur of motion one woman likened to hummingbird's wings.

"Enough!" Slocum said. "At least keep your goddamn

voices down so the man that was shot doesn't have to hear about what a thrilling spectacle it was."

The crowd bowed their heads at the same time as if they'd just received a command from their preacher during Sunday mass. When the door to the office was opened, the air was still enough for the creak of the hinges to be clearly heard.

Slocum turned to find the doctor stepping outside, using a bloody rag to clean off his hands. "How's he doing, Doc?" Slocum asked.

"He's dying, that's how he's doing."

"Then shouldn't you be in there with him?"

"There's nothing left for me to do," the doctor replied. "Besides, he asked to see you."

"Me?"

"You're John Slocum?"

"Yes."

"Then it's you. I'd suggest you step lively."

Slocum walked past the doctor and into the grimy little office. Seeing the lawman lying there with his wooden leg on prominent display put a lot of things into perspective. It also cast the man in a whole new light. What made Slocum feel even worse was the fact that he truly hadn't gotten to know Sheriff Cass before writing him off as a lazy waste of a badge.

Not wanting to be disrespectful by towering over the wounded man, Slocum got down on one knee and said, "The doctor told me you wanted to speak to me, but I don't think . . ."

"Don't think . . . what?" Cass asked. "Don't think . . . I got enough sense. . . . to remember your name?"

"No. I was just going to say I thought you'd want to speak to someone else. Maybe your wife or family?"

"Ain't got none of . . . either."

Cass was dying. Of that, there was no doubt. Slocum could see as much in the lawman's chalky face or in Cass's eyes, which were hazy and wandering as if he was seeing things that no living man could see. By Slocum's reckoning, the lawman could pass at any moment.

"Find them, Slocum," Cass said.

"The old man who shot you?"

The lawman nodded although it obviously hurt like hell for him to do so. "Him and Bensonn. After I was shot, my jail keys were taken from me like I was some kinda damn baby. Ain't felt so helpless . . . since I got my leg blown off. And you're right . . . about me not doin' my job."

"No," Slocum said quickly. "I spoke out of turn with that. I was just . . ." He stopped when he felt a firm grip around one wrist.

The sheriff grabbed hold of Slocum's arm as if it was the only thing preventing him from falling into the abyss. "You were speakin' yer mind, and it was the truth. If I couldn't carry out my duties . . . I should have . . . turned in my badge. I asked you here so I could keep doin' my job. The man that killed me . . . his name is Far Eye."

"Is that an Indian name?" Slocum asked.

"No . . . that's just what folks call him. He freed Bensonn and will probably be. . . . movin' on to Spencer Flats."

"They told you all that before shooting you?"

"No, Rob was talking . . . talking up a storm when he was . . . in the cell. Heard something . . . about Spencer Flats. He was my responsibility. Goin' after them both should'a been my job, but I . . . probably would've let it slide. That's why . . . I'm deputizing you."

Slocum pulled his arm away from the dying man's reach. "Oh, no. I'm no bounty hunter and I'm no lawman."

"You . . . could've fooled me." Until Cass allowed his head to fall down and thump against the floor, Slocum hadn't realized he'd been holding it up. In fact, when he lay back, Cass relaxed most of his muscles to the point that his body looked like a water skin with its contents leaking out through a small hole. His eyes were open and fixed on a point directly above him. When he spoke, it was with a voice that seemed to be a hundred miles away. "I wanted to do one last thing . . . one part of my duty that could make up for . . . all I let slide. You don't know me well . . . enough to avenge me and you ain't kin. I thought . . . maybe . . . you could clean up the mess I'm about to leave behind."

Slocum pulled in a deep breath and let it out. "You say the name of the town is Spencer Flats?"

Cass nodded weakly. "Stars . . ."

"Are you seeing the stars?" Slocum asked quietly.

Suddenly, Cass snapped his eyes open and stared directly at him. "The star's in my top drawer you . . . damn fool! Take . . ."

And then he was gone.

Slocum stood up, walked over to the sheriff's desk, and opened the top drawer. Among other things such as papers, some pencils, and a few mismatched pistol rounds was a small deputy's badge in desperate need of polishing. He took the little star and placed it in his pocket. All that remained was for him to tell the doctor what had happened.

There was no need to rush.

6

When Slocum returned to his room at the Split Log, he immediately gathered up his things and stuffed them into his saddlebags. Tess showed up before he was through, breathlessly storming through the door. "Didn't you see me downstairs?" she asked.

"Guess not."

"I was asking about what happened and I heard the sheriff was shot. I thought I'd go down and have a look, but knew you'd be there and would probably just tell me to go back."

"And?"

"And . . . I went anyway. But I didn't see much."

Slocum nodded, hearing what he'd expected to hear from her. He didn't have much in the way of belongings, so it wasn't long before his saddlebags were filled and hefted over one shoulder. Turning toward the door, he was stopped by a perturbed blond barrier.

"So you're leaving?" she asked.

"Looks that way."

"Do I get to know why?"

Slocum planted his feet and growled, "Did you think I

was going to look for a nice piece of land, build a house, and stay here?"

"No. I just thought you'd tell me before you rode off!"

Once again, Slocum felt like an ass. Even though that was becoming an unwelcome habit, he wasn't getting used to it. "Sorry, Tess. You're right. I just . . . I watched a man die today. That's not the sort of thing that sets well with me no matter how many damn times I have to do it."

"The sheriff?"

He nodded.

Her expression softened and she approached Slocum to gently rub the side of his arm. "I'm sorry. Did you know him?"

"Not as such. In fact, I wouldn't have had anything good to say about him if you asked me that question a little while ago. I still can't say I know him . . ." Slocum winced and added, "Knew him . . . very well, but he wasn't a bad man. I guess I've run across so many lawmen that were crooked, inept, or just plain worthless that my opinion of the whole lot has been sullied. In any event, this one didn't deserve to be gunned down like a dog in his own front door."

"Nobody deserves that," Tess said reverently.

"Actually," he chuckled, "some deserve it or worse. This one didn't. He asked me to do something for him before he died and I'm inclined to do it."

Tess wrapped her arms around him and hugged Slocum as best she could with the bulky bags hanging off one shoulder. "That's because you're a good man, John. If you'd like, I can wait here for when you're done."

"You better not wait," he told her. "I don't know how long it'll take. For all I know, the bit of information he gave me won't lead anywhere. Or it could lead to somewhere in another direction entirely. When I'm through with this, it's best I move along. That's what I was set to do before long anyway. You were, too, unless I'm mistaken."

"You're right. I've got things to do as well." She held him at arm's length and smiled warmly while taking in the sight of him. "Fulfilling a dying man's wish. You're such a good man."

"I'm a sucker for a sob story," he said. "This isn't the first time it's gotten me into trouble and it probably won't be the last."

"Maybe there won't be any trouble."

"There's always trouble."

Slocum collected his horse, saddled up, and rode out of town. Once Tarnish Mills was behind him, it was easy enough to focus on what lay ahead. All he had to go on were a few hints given by a dead man. Some could have been useless. Since dying men frequently spoke nonsense in their last few moments on earth, everything Sheriff Cass had said could have been worthless. As Slocum rode along a wooded trail leading toward higher country, he questioned his judgment on accepting the job in the first place.

It was easy to be swayed at the right moment, especially when emotions were running high. Then there was the fact that he simply felt bad for having given the lawman a tough time. Slocum started to chuckle.

He'd known plenty of men who'd been injured a lot worse than Cass in the war. Soldiers missing both legs, an arm or two, or any combination thereof tended to become tougher. The quickest way to piss one of those men off was to treat him like a helpless child in need of pity. Soldiers who were still trudging forward in their lives after surviving battle and the horrors of an amputation table were unlike normal men. They were stronger in spirit and harder than iron. Showing outward signs of pity toward men like that was a good way to get a crutch buried into some very delicate anatomy. Cass had survived his own hell and had become a functioning lawman. Perhaps he'd gotten a little lax in his efforts, but that didn't mean he was a pathetic creature who couldn't handle the harsh words Slocum had thrown at him. So Slocum allowed himself to let it go.

Now that he was no longer feeling guilty, he thought about why he was heading out after two outlaws he barely knew. It wasn't because of guilt or any sense of owing Cass anything. Something needed to be done and he was the man to do it.

That was it.

That was all he needed.

And that, Slocum decided, was the last time he would look back.

According to the liveryman in town who'd given him directions, Spencer Flats was still about another twenty or so miles in front of him.

Fortunately, those were some beautiful miles. Perhaps witnessing one man's last day on earth made Slocum more appreciative of such things. He soaked up the sights of all those trees and the sloping, rocky terrain beneath his horse's hooves. If not for a washed-out bridge spanning a wide river, he might have made it all the way to town that day. Instead, he was forced to find another spot to cross several miles down the shore. That ate up a portion of the day's remaining sunlight and put Spencer Flats effectively out of reach for the time being. Slocum found a good spot to build a fire, and after he'd eaten a supper of some salty ham and a can of pears, he stretched out and gazed up at the stars.

It wasn't too much longer before the day caught up to him in a rush. Once he grew too tired to keep his eyes open, he was snoring peacefully.

The next morning, Slocum moved like a well-oiled machine. With nobody along to talk or share a chore, he set about the task of breaking camp, preparing his horse for the day's ride, and moving along. In some respects, it was quicker than if he had anyone there to help. Solitude meant there was no one around to complain, and that wasn't a bad thing. It was early enough for the sun to be bright without being hot, which left the day spread out in front of him like a beautiful, richly colored blanket.

It wasn't all the time that Slocum got a chance to take in his surroundings just for the sheer enjoyment of what they had to offer. All too often, he was running away from something or running to something else. There was a sense of urgency in completing the job he'd taken on, but he wasn't worried about getting it done. He had an ace in his pocket and its name was Rob Bensonn.

Wherever Rob stopped, he would start talking. Since he'd been busted out of a jail cell, he would want to boast about that more than anything. If he was in the company of someone who'd gunned down a lawman to get him out of that jail, Rob would have some things to say about that as well. Even if Rob was enjoying lunch in a room full of folks who didn't give a damn who he was or where he was headed, he'd still have plenty to say. As long as he kept flapping his gums, someone would hear. All Slocum had to do was find one or two locals whose ears were in proper working order and he would be pointed in the right direction.

When Rob made another mistake, Slocum would find out about it one way or another. Besides, these weren't the first men he'd hunted. Normally, he had much less to go on and he had faith in himself that he would find this man as well. Without that faith in himself, he would have been dead a long time ago.

Having covered so much ground the previous day, Slocum caught his first glimpse of Spencer Flats well before noon. It was nestled in some rocky hills and a thick wall of pines to the north. Slocum followed the circling trail until he was set on a course that put the town directly in front of him. It was only then that he pulled back on the reins.

Until now, Slocum had been cautious. He was always cautious. The caution needed when hunting a killer, on the other hand, was a whole different animal. Even though he'd been trying to come up with something that might help his cause, the name *Far Eye* hadn't struck a chord. All he knew was what the witnesses to Sheriff Cass's murder had told him, which was that the gunman was fast on the draw and had deadly aim. The freshly dug grave back in Tarnish Mills proved that much. And if a man as dangerous as that truly was bound for Spencer Flats, that meant Slocum had a new batch of worries to consider.

During this entire ride, both yesterday and today, he hadn't seen anything to make him think he was being followed. If Rob or his murderous partner had caught up with him, they would have made a move by now. That, however, was no reason to mosey into a strange town when he could be spotted from any number of angles.

Slocum was looking straight down the trail to what appeared to be a main street through the town ahead. Trees surrounded the perimeter of the settlement along a sloping wall of rock to the east. The western edge of town was along a thin patch of woods. Slocum guessed he could get into Spencer Flats from that side without much trouble. He veered away from the trail and made his way through trees that formed a barrier which grew thicker every twenty yards or so. Before the trees became impassable, they thinned out to reveal another trail. This one wasn't nearly as wide or well worn as the one he'd previously used, but his stallion was able to traverse it without brushing against too many branches. The trees thinned out quickly. More than likely, they'd been cleared away to provide lumber used to build the houses that were gathered in clusters on this side of town.

After emerging from the trees, he was spotted almost immediately by a boy with sandy brown hair, striking blue eyes, and limbs that were skinny as string beans.

"Howdy," Slocum said to the boy.

The kid looked back at him with his mouth hanging open.

"Just passing through," Slocum said.

Before he could get past the kid, he heard, "I ain't supposed to talk to strangers."

"That's fine, then. I'll be on my way."

"What's your name?"

"Aren't you supposed to steer clear of strangers?" Slocum asked.

The kid shook his head and scratched at his hip. "I just ain't supposed to talk to 'em. I'm James."

"Pleased to meet you, James."

"You know them other men that come into town?"

"I don't know. I imagine plenty of men come through here."

Without hesitation, the boy replied, "No they don't. You look like one of them."

"I do?"

James kept up with the easy pace of Slocum's horse. With one hand, he stroked the stallion's side before reaching toward the boot containing Slocum's rifle. "You look like 'em on account of all the guns you're carrying. Them other men were carrying guns, too."

"Most men carry guns when they travel," Slocum said. "For snakes and such."

"Them others were different. They weren't huntin' and they weren't cowboys."

"You certain of that?"

"Yes sir, I am," James said proudly. "I watch everyone that comes and goes."

"That must keep you busy."

James shrugged. "School ain't starting for another week and there ain't many men that come through here."

"That's right," Slocum chuckled. "So you said. Have you seen enough men with guns to tell the hunters and cowboys from the rest?"

After thinking about that while walking alongside Slocum's horse, James winced and said, "I suppose not. All I know is that cowboys and hunters come into town using one of the main trails and they usually ain't alone. Them other two could be cowboys, I guess."

"What made you think they were different?"

"On account of what one of the men said. He could'a just been talking, I suppose."

Trying not to appear as interested as he was, Slocum asked, "What was he talking about?"

"They was putting their horses up at my pa's stable and one of them said he shouldn't have to pay because he's a damn killer and that this whole town's lucky he don't burn it down."

"Best watch the cussing, kid," Slocum warned. "Your ma might hear."

James took a quick look over his shoulder and lowered his voice to a whisper. "My pa said them men are gunmen or outlaws."

"And you thought I was an outlaw, too?"

"No," the boy said as his cheeks flushed. "But I figured you might be a gunman seeing as how you snuck into town the way you did."

"You've got a good eye, James." Seeing the way the boy gasped, Slocum quickly added, "But I'm no outlaw. Can you do me a favor?"

"Maybe."

"Introduce me to your pa."

The stable at the end of Main Street was marked by a simple sign with the words STALLS FOR RENT & HORSES FOR SALE painted in block letters. James led the way and Slocum followed with his head angled downward just enough for the brim of his hat to keep most of his face from being seen by casual observers. Fortunately, the town was quiet and there weren't many observers, casual or otherwise, to worry about. Anyone looking down from the few buildings along the street would only see a boy leading a man and a horse to a stable. Nothing eye-catching about that.

At least, that's what Slocum hoped.

When they got within a few yards of the stable's large twin doors, James broke into a run and hollered, "Pa! Pa! I brought someone to see you."

Slocum resisted the temptation to look around for anyone taking interest in the short but suddenly loud procession.

The man who stepped out to greet the boy wore battered jeans and a heavy blacksmith's apron over a rumpled red and black checked shirt. It was plain to see where James got his height, but any string bean qualities the older man might have possessed had long since worn away. He clapped his boy on the shoulder and left his hand in place to keep James from bouncing around any further. "No need for shouting, son. You'll scare away a customer. That is," he added while showing Slocum a crooked smile, "if you're here about renting a stall."

"I am, sir," Slocum said. "But I'd also like to ask about some other customers you might have had lately."

The liveryman studied Slocum in much the same way his son had not too long ago. Like the boy, his eyes snagged on the weapons Slocum carried. His pockmarked face shifted beneath a thick beard, making his entire demeanor seem darker when he asked, "They friends of yours?"

Slocum shook his head. "Not hardly, sir." Then he peeled open his jacket to reveal the deputy's badge he'd pinned to his shirt a few miles outside of town. The rusty star may have been small, but it made a world of difference to the liveryman.

"You out to haul them two away from here?" the liveryman asked.

"One way or another."

The other man's grin returned. "Then I may be able to help you."

7

The liveryman's name was Andrew. Once he saw Slocum's badge, he was more than happy to introduce himself, show Slocum around the stable, and answer any questions he could. Slocum wasn't accustomed to someone being so cooperative without persuasion in the form of money or a threat. Either Andrew was a good man trying to do the right thing or he was shining Slocum on and setting him up for something else farther down the road. Although he drifted more toward the former of those possibilities, Slocum had acquired too many knife wounds in the back to discount the latter.

"So the two men that rode these horses," Slocum said while gazing at a pair of stalls near the back of the stable. "They just arrived?"

"Late last night, yes sir," Andrew replied.

"What did they look like?"

Even though he wasn't much for words, Andrew rattled off a good enough description of Rob. As for the other man, Andrew simply said he was old and had a full head of silver hair.

"And you think they're gunmen?" Slocum asked.

"They were both carrying guns and both knew how to use 'em. I served six years in the army, so I've seen plenty of men carrying guns. The ones who enjoy pulling the trigger are easy to spot. These men had that look in their eyes."

Slocum knew that look all too well. "Where did they go after leaving here?"

"I recommended they try one of the hotels in town. My wife rents out one of the rooms in our house, but I didn't want them two assholes anywhere near my family."

Upon hearing his father curse, James laughed. He stopped the instant Andrew fixed him with a cold, hard glare.

"So when will the rest of the lawmen be coming?" the liveryman asked.

"Can't say as there will be any others," Slocum replied.

"That's a deputy's badge. Weren't you sent by a sheriff or marshal or someone like that?"

"I was. He was killed."

"That's a right shame, mister," Andrew said in a genuinely heartfelt tone. "Are you from anywhere nearby?"

Slocum's first instinct was to be honest with Andrew since the liveryman seemed like a good man. However, there was more to consider than the other man's character when he told him, "I'm from a town about three days west from here. Are you familiar with the territory?"

"Not that part of it."

Since that meant less lying to Andrew, Slocum was glad to hear it. "Do you get much word from other towns?"

"Not as such. Folks that pass through here do their fair amount of talking, but I don't listen to what don't concern me. Plenty of men make their rounds to sell or trade. You can find them at Jocelyn's."

"Does she own a restaurant or saloon?"

"Jocelyn's is the name of a saloon. Biggest one in town. You go there and ask around and you'll hear plenty of news from neighboring towns. As for me, I got my own work to do."

"Pa always says he knows well enough the rest of the world is rotten to the core so he don't want to hear about it."

Rubbing his hand on the top of his son's head in a way that seemed awfully similar to covering James's mouth, Andrew snapped, "Enough of that, son. This man don't need to hear what goes on at home."

"He'll hear it if he's renting Aunt Sally's room." Turning hopeful eyes toward Slocum, James asked, "You are renting her room, ain't you?"

"It'd probably be best if I didn't stay at one of them hotels," Slocum said. "It might be best if I camped somewhere outside of town where I'd be out of sight."

"My boy may talk a lot," Andrew said, "but he says some smart things. He also knows when to keep his mouth shut, so he won't go spreading any word about you being here. Right, son?"

"Yes sir," James immediately replied.

Andrew nodded proudly. "If a lawman needs someplace to rest his head while doing his job, he's more'n welcome in my home. As far as staying out of sight, nobody's got to know you're here. Folks around these parts know better than to poke their noses in my affairs."

"I'm sure they do. I'll take the room."

"All right, then. Who should I tell my wife is coming?"

Slocum extended his hand and introduced himself. He'd already put enough faith in Andrew, so he wasn't going to insult him by giving him an assumed name.

"Pleased to meet you, John. James, take him to his room."

"Yes sir."

James led him back to within twenty paces of the spot where Slocum had breached the tree line while entering town. The house was a large, two-floor structure with a porch wrapping all the way around. Inside, the furnishings were solid. No doubt, either Andrew or another family member had fashioned them personally. The walls were decorated with a few Bible verses stitched onto plain white cloth within simple wooden frames. Despite looking like it belonged on a piece of sprawling Texas land, the house was a warm, inviting place maintained by a stout woman who was only about an inch taller than her son. She greeted Slocum with a warm, friendly smile.

"You're here about the room?" she asked.

"That's right, ma'am."

"Well, don't just stand there," she said to James. "Show our guest upstairs!"

"If it's all the same to you, I'd like to tend to some business in town," Slocum said.

She nodded and swatted James on the backside to get him moving up the stairs. "We'll have everything ready for you when you get back. Supper's at six sharp."

"I hope to make it, ma'am, but please don't take offense if I'm unable."

She tried to wave off Slocum's words, but her smile ran a little too deep and her eyes lingered on him for just a bit too long. He wouldn't go so far as to say she would step out of line if given a chance, but Slocum believed her when she said she'd save a scrap or two for him from the dinner table.

He tipped his hat and excused himself from the house. As soon as he was outside, it was straight back to business. He hadn't ridden into Spencer Flats to make friends. There were killers about and he meant to make them answer for however many lives they'd taken. For one of those lives in particular, they would pay dearly. Just to be safe, Slocum removed the badge from his shirt and tucked it into a pocket. Folks tended to treat lawmen differently, and many weren't as accommodating as Andrew.

Although Jocelyn's was about the size of a small house, it wasn't much more than a large tent draped over a wooden frame. The bar was solid oak with a polished rail, which made it seem more than a little out of place surrounded by tables and chairs that could have been dropped from covered wagons after not having been tied down properly.

At first, it seemed as if there was nobody tending the bar. Slocum approached it and was about to rap his knuckles upon the surface when a dark-skinned woman with thick black hair poked her head up from behind the bar just high enough to be seen. She had large brown eyes and skin that had the texture of molasses. She seemed to be somewhere in her forties, but could have looked younger if her hair hadn't been tied back into a tight, severe bun.

"I will be right with you," she said in an accent that was three parts British and one part . . . something else.

Slocum waited patiently after she disappeared once more beneath the bar. Soon, the beer taps sticking up like polished metal stems began to tremble. Along with the clanging of metal on metal, her voice rolled up from below. Even when she swore six ways to Sunday, her voice still managed to sound cultured. Leaning forward, Slocum asked, "Need a hand?"

"Do you know anything about unclogging one of these pipes?"

"Not as such, but I imagine I could figure something out."

"I can figure something out as well," she said without bothering to look up from where she struggled to work. "You just stay put and tell Haresh what you want."

The man who approached Slocum moved so silently that he could very well have appeared from thin air. His skin was slightly lighter in color than hers, but was still dark as if bronzed from years in the sun. He stood a full head taller than Slocum and was built more solidly than most of the homes in town. Scowling down at him through a thin, charcoal-colored beard, he stood like a redwood and waited for Slocum's order.

Without missing a beat, Slocum knuckled one of the taps and said, "I'll have a beer."

Haresh's face cracked like a parched desert floor into a narrow grin.

"There's a special hell for smart alecks," the woman said from beneath the bar.

"Then how about a whiskey?" Slocum asked.

Moving like a tiger, Haresh circled around the bar, found a bottle, and poured a drink. When he set the glass down in front of Slocum, he did so with a smooth, barely noticeable flourish of one hand.

"You're not from around here, are you?" Slocum asked as he picked up his drink.

After one more curse delivered in her richly textured accent, the woman grunted and finally got something beneath the bar to move the way she wanted it to move. Instead of metallic screeching, the pipes made a smoother sound that went all the way up through the wood of the bar. She stood up, tried the tap, and beamed when the beer started to flow. "Now that is ingenuity brought all the way from Nepal!"

"Inflicted upon American craftsmanship," Haresh growled.

"I'd argue if it wasn't true," Slocum said while lifting his glass.

The woman wiped her hands upon a towel that was looped over the thin belt encircling her waist just above her dark brown skirts. "I apologize, sir. That is no way to talk about such a fine country."

"I'll drink to that also," Slocum said, "as soon as I have some beer."

She picked up a mug, shook out some water that had collected in the bottom, and then filled it with beer. Although there were some bits of sediment swirling inside, Slocum had definitely seen much worse. He took the glass, raised it, and proclaimed, "To fine countries far and wide."

"Cheers!" both the woman and Haresh said in unison.

The beer went down easy and left a pleasant, grainy

aftertaste. Slocum took another long sip and then held the glass at arm's length so he could inspect it. "That's not what I was expecting," he said.

The woman raised her eyebrows. "Is that a good or bad thing?"

After another sip followed by a careful series of lip smacking, Slocum told her, "I think . . . good. Yes. A good thing."

"Then, since you so good-naturedly drank the glass intended only to clean out my pipes, you should enjoy your next one even more."

Haresh chuckled and took the mostly empty glass Slocum had set down. When he dumped it out into a basin behind the bar, the big man did so as if he didn't want to get any of the beer on his hands. The next glass was filled with beer that had the color of tanned leather and had considerably less sediment inside. Slocum sampled it tentatively.

"Well?" she asked. "Am I right?"

"I hate to admit it, but you're right," Slocum told her. "Much better."

"What's so hard to admit? That perfection can be poured into a glass?"

"I just don't appreciate being tricked into drinking something you meant to throw out."

Waving an impatient hand toward Haresh, she said, "That one's fussy as well. He won't drink from these spigots until I'm midway through a keg, and even then, it's only if the temperature is just right in here. You should see him on a hot day. Insufferable."

"I just know what I like," Haresh grunted.

Using a clean cloth to polish the curved pipes of the taps, the barkeep asked, "Does it make you feel better knowing that both of those drinks are on the house?"

"Yes," Slocum said with a smile. "Much." He drained almost half of his glass in one sip, tasting hints of exotic

flavors that were difficult to nail down. Since he wasn't aiming to figure out her recipes, he simply enjoyed letting the
drink flow through his system.

Perhaps responding to the blissful look on his face, the
bartender said, "No more are free, you know. I have a business to run."

"I'm here on business as well," Slocum said. "Have there
been any strangers in town recently?"

"Besides you?" Haresh asked.

"Yes. Strangers with big mouths."

"You mean . . . besides you?"

Slocum turned to lean sideways against the bar so he
could face the big man directly. Haresh's thick hair was
darker than wet coal and covered his scalp like a helmet.
The whiskers on his face, too long to be stubble and too
short to be a beard, looked instead like something that had
been sketched onto his chin and cheeks with a black pencil.
His teeth were brilliant white and he flashed them at Slocum
like a predator grinning at its prey.

"Do we have a problem I didn't know about?" Slocum
asked.

"That's just his paltry attempt at humor," the bartender
said.

"Yes," Haresh added. "If there was a problem between
you and I, you would know it."

Slocum decided to take them at their word, but allowed
his warning glare to linger on Haresh for a few more seconds before shifting his gaze back to the bartender. "Anyway, I'm looking for information about any strangers that
have come to town recently."

"How recent?" she asked.

"Anytime in the last couple of days. Maybe even yesterday or earlier today. I was told that you might know about
any new arrivals."

"I would. Perhaps you should have a word with those two
men right over there." With that, she pointed to the table in

the farthest corner of the saloon. In a structure that was mostly canvas wrapped around a wooden frame, it was the most secure place to be, barricaded with wooden posts on one side, a tall support post on another, and a few tables scattered in the space that remained. The men hadn't been there before, so Slocum assumed they'd snuck in when he'd been sampling the beer. One of the men looked to be about the right size and weight of Rob Bensonn, but both were wrapped in so many layers of clothing that it was difficult to see much more than that. They even wore large dusty hats on their heads and had bandannas tied around their necks in a rumpled mass obscuring them even further.

"When did they arrive?" Slocum asked, suddenly becoming aware of just how much voices carried within the glorified tent.

"Don't know," she told him. "But they look like strangers to me."

Haresh smirked.

"Any others?" Slocum asked.

She lowered her voice as well. Leaning forward, she said, "There were a few men that came through yesterday. I didn't get much of a look at them because I only heard about it from the woman who runs the boardinghouse. We both steer business each other's way and she told me that two men came fresh off the trail."

"Does she know where they came from?"

"No. Apparently, they're the quiet types. To be honest, most strangers are quiet around here."

Haresh spoke in a low rumble that barely got his lips moving. "If men ride through who look like they use their guns to kill something other than supper, odds are they're either outlaws or vigilantes. Both kinds are trouble."

That made plenty of sense to Slocum, and as he listened, he weighed the benefits of showing his badge. Considering the fact that many vigilantes only wanted to be deputized as a way to make their killings legal, he opted to keep things the way they were. "Any chance you might back me up?" he asked Haresh.

The bigger man furrowed his brow and looked at Slocum as if he were doing so from a hundred feet in the air. "A man who is looking for backup is usually also looking for trouble."

"Not looking for it," Slocum corrected. "But there may be some. Since this is your place, I thought you might like to take part in keeping things civil."

"Everything will be civil enough if they sit there, and you," Haresh said while dropping a hand that felt like a lead weight onto Slocum's shoulder, "stay right here."

When Slocum looked to her for support, the bartender said, "I'm afraid I will have to agree with him."

"I don't believe I caught your name."

"Didn't you read the sign above the door? I'm Jocelyn."

"And I'm John Slocum."

"John Slocum?" Haresh growled. "I have heard that name before." He looked to Jocelyn and said, "This one is trouble."

"Did you hear about what happened in Tarnish Mills?" Slocum asked. "It's a town not too far from—"

"I know where it is," Jocelyn cut in. "And if you're talking about Sheriff Cass being killed, I heard about that, too. Not too long ago, in fact, from a silverware merchant making his rounds through this territory. Do those two men over there have anything to do with what happened to Sheriff Cass?"

"I don't know yet," Slocum replied. "Won't know until I go over there and have a word with them."

"You will recognize them when you see their faces?" Haresh asked.

"At least one of them."

"Then just get them to turn around."

"And if they recognize me," Slocum replied, "which at

least one of them will, they could very well start shooting. You want that?"

Both Jocelyn and Haresh looked at the rest of the saloon. There were only a few other customers scattered around the place, but there was plenty of movement outside. Shadows drifted back and forth along three of the four walls. Since those walls were made of canvas, any stray bullets could very easily find a home in any one of the folks passing by.

"I don't want trouble," Jocelyn hissed.

"If those men aren't who I think they are, there won't be any trouble," Slocum told her.

"And if they are?"

"Then there was bound to be trouble sooner or later. I've always preferred to get it out of the way before it brews into something worse."

Surprisingly enough, Haresh said, "I agree." With that, he reached across the bar to feel under it until he found a shotgun. At first, the weapon looked like any number of shotguns kept behind any number of bars in saloons around the world. But when Slocum took a closer look, he realized the weapon was twice as big as he'd thought and looked normal only because it was being held in a pair of massive hands.

"Good Lord!" Slocum wheezed. "You hunt bear with that thing?"

Gripping a gun that would have looked like a cannon in anyone else's hands, Haresh said, "Yes."

"All right, then. This should be easy." Knowing better than to give the bigger man orders, Slocum thanked his stars Haresh was on his side and moseyed toward the table that had caught his eye.

So far, the men sitting there had yet to do much of anything but talk quietly among themselves. Although there wasn't anything particularly suspicious about that, Slocum didn't like the way they kept their eyes glued to the front half of the room, where a large flap next to the door was held open as a window. Slocum's hand drifted toward the Colt holstered at his hip, but only to rest upon its grip. When he approached the table, he meant to get as close as he could before they noticed without startling them badly enough for them to draw on him out of pure instinct. It was a narrow line to walk, but this wasn't Slocum's first attempt at it.

When he was over halfway to the table, Slocum allowed his boots to knock against the floor a little louder. The boards were merely laid upon the ground beneath the tent, but he made enough noise to get one of the men to glance back at him. He was an older gentleman with gray hair and a face lined by his years on this earth. Actually, Slocum decided to hold off on thinking of him as a gentleman until he got a look at the man's companion.

Apparently, the next man to step into Jocelyn's didn't share those reservations.

"Gentlemen!" he announced as he strode inside and positioned himself with his back to the wooden posts separating the window from the door. "And . . . lady. I would kindly ask that you remain where you are so that I may have a word with these two skunks." Fixing his eyes onto the men seated at the table in front of Slocum, he added, "The pair of you will save yourselves some pain if you step outside without a fuss."

8

The new arrival had silver hair that was cut short enough to look like bristles on a fancy brush. He was modest in height, but not in dress. His pearl gray suit was freshly pressed and was accented nicely by the silver watch chain crossing his midsection. A double-rig holster strapped around his waist and made from tooled leather was worn down to a consistency that would move with him like any other part of his body. Slocum couldn't see the guns kept in that holster because of the suit jacket covering them, but he had caught a glimpse of highly polished steel or maybe even silver. The man's eyes were pointed directly at the two sitting at the table in front of Slocum.

Both men seated there pushed away from the table and stood up. "Who the hell are you?" the gray-haired one asked.

"I've heard you've been asking around about me," the well-dressed man at the front of the saloon replied. "My name is Ferril Abernathy."

The other man who'd been seated at the table in Slocum's sights hunched forward as if he was about to cover the distance between himself and the front door in one jump. "You're Far Eye Abernathy?"

"Yes," the silver-haired man replied as if he'd been born for that moment. "I most certainly am. And I believe you two are Matt and Paul Southard?"

By now, Slocum had circled around the table so he could get a better look at the men seated there. From his new vantage point, he could tell the second man was younger than the first but wasn't Rob Bensonn.

"I can tell you men are anxious," Abernathy said. "Please know that I did not come here to fight. If you push me, however, I will defend myself."

"If you didn't want a fight, you shouldn't have called us out," one of the Southards replied. The older one.

"I came here to face you like a man. It is you who have been hunting me down like an animal."

"You *are* an animal! You killed a Kansas lawman in cold blood."

"I didn't ask for that fight either," Abernathy replied in a manner that was so flippant it grated against Slocum's nerves. "I'm giving you this chance to leave me in peace."

"Just like you gave Sheriff Cass a chance?" the older Southard asked.

"That's right," Abernathy said.

The younger Southard gritted his teeth and snarled, "Fuck you and your goddamn chances!"

Abernathy remained poised, even as his right hand snapped toward his holster and brought his gun up from its spot at his side. The pistol glinted in the sunlight pouring in through the door and window as it barked twice in quick succession. Both men at the table leapt aside, but the younger one tripped over his chair and fell to the floor. The older man dropped to one knee while flipping his table over. That way, a good portion of his body was shielded as he unleashed some return fire from his pistol.

In this time, Slocum hadn't stood idle. First, he dove for

cover behind one of the other tables. He could hear the customers storming toward the rear of the saloon, where Jocelyn shouted for them to join her behind the bar. Slocum drew his Colt, but was unable to fire before a series of gunshots drove him behind cover. Peeking around the other side of the table, Slocum was just able to catch a glimpse of Abernathy before another round drilled through the table less than an inch away from his face.

The silver-haired man at the front door stood his ground while wearing an expression that was so calm it bordered on being sleepy. Both of his hands were wrapped around a pistol. Normally, that kind of showboating was left for over-eager kids who didn't know any better or fools. Abernathy was neither. He surveyed the saloon like a man who'd cast his eyes upon a thousand battlefields and pulled his triggers to unleash a flurry of lead that somehow found its mark. Slocum may have taken action in the next fraction of a second, but that time was cut even shorter as more bullets chipped away at the table he used for cover.

He'd seen plenty of men who were fast with their guns.

He'd seen a few shooters who could accomplish feats with bullets that were damn near inspired.

What Slocum hadn't seen was someone who combined those two gifts as handily as Ferril Abernathy.

The only thing that put a kink in the savvy shooter's plan was a deafening roar from Haresh's shotgun. A single blast ripped through the air, making Slocum wonder if the entire saloon had gone up in flames. Having reflexively dropped to the floor, Slocum picked himself up again as splintered fragments of the tables around him fluttered like insects on all sides.

Abernathy had stopped firing, but not because he'd been dropped by the shotgun blast. He was gone. The front portion of the saloon was empty. Judging by where most of the damage had been inflicted, the shotgun had been pointed to the right and above the door instead of directly at it.

"Damn!" Haresh snapped as he reloaded the shotgun. "There were too many of you in here to risk a straight shot. He got away."

"The hell he did," Slocum said as he grabbed the table lying in front of him and used it to pull himself to his feet. Since he wasn't about to underestimate someone with Abernathy's skills, Slocum assumed charging out the front door would only give him a quick trip to the hereafter. So he set his sights on the closest wall, drew his knife from its scabbard at his boot, and used a powerful downward slash to cut through the canvas. The opening wasn't quite big enough to accommodate him, but the momentum behind his body was enough to widen the tear as he shoved through.

Slocum stepped outside with his gun at the ready to find Abernathy strolling casually away. The older man's steps were confident, his back was straight, and he even paused to tip his hat to the occasional local woman gawking at him from a safe distance.

"Where do you think you're going?" Slocum called out.

Abernathy turned, narrowed his eyes, and fired twice. Slocum barely saw the other man's arm rise, but he sure as hell felt the lead whip past him. Guessing that the other man's impressive skills with a shooting iron hadn't been pure luck, Slocum glanced back to see if Abernathy had been aiming at something behind him. Sure enough, the younger Southard gnashed his teeth while struggling to bring his pistol up to bear. Any strength he had to complete the motion leaked out through the fresh hole that had been blasted into his chest. He let out a pained grunt, dropped his gun, and keeled over.

"What about me?" Slocum shouted.

"Fight's not with you, sir," Abernathy replied. "I suggest you count that as a stroke of good luck and be on your way."

Slocum stood his ground as heavy steps thumped against the floor behind him. A few seconds later, Haresh stepped through the rip in the canvas wall and snarled, "You will just let him leave?"

"He'll be looking for me to follow him. Running after him now will only play into his strength."

"What strength?"

"He killed that man pretty handily," Slocum said while waving back toward the younger Southard's body. "Expecting him to miss someone rushing after him is taking one hell of a stupid gamble if you ask me."

"What else is there?"

"Any law around here?"

"Volunteers. One old man and a fellow who won't do anything if it involves taking him away from his family."

Slocum holstered his Colt. "Then let's try to give him a surprise before he gets out of town."

Haresh grinned. "So you do mean to chase him?"

"Of course. You think I'll let someone kill another man right in front of me?"

"Cut down that alley there," Haresh said while pointing to the narrow passage between two nearby buildings. "I'll circle around the other way."

All Slocum could do was take the path he'd been given and hope his partner wouldn't let him down. The buildings across the street weren't much more than large shacks and formed an awfully short alley. Slocum rushed through it in no time, and when he emerged at the other side, he came face to face with a familiar and very angry son of a bitch.

"Howdy," Rob Bensonn said as he fired a hasty shot from the Winchester in his hands.

The shot went wide and Slocum drew his Colt. Less than a fraction of a second later, he fired from the hip. Not only did his bullet fail to draw blood, but it also failed to make Rob back off or even jump aside. Instead, the outlaw stood his ground wearing a wide, sloppy smile.

"Should've left good enough alone," Rob said while levering another round. "Just like in Tarnish Mills, huh? Guess you're just the sort who keeps chasing after things that don't concern them. Do that too long and it'll be the death of you. Just like today!"

Slocum let the other man speak his piece. A small reason for that was the off chance that Rob might actually say something worth hearing. The biggest reason, however, was to give Slocum enough time to square his shoulders, line up his shot, and take a chance of his own. When he saw that Rob was about to fire his rifle, Slocum got ready to squeeze his own trigger, but before Rob's Winchester had a chance to respond, another shot was fired from higher ground to drop Bensonn straight to the dirt.

"Wh-What happened?" Rob stammered.

Slocum kept the Colt aimed at him as he moved to Rob's side. One boot lowered onto the Winchester to pin the rifle, along with one of the hands holding it, flat against the ground. Whoever had fired the final shot had been well hidden and was most definitely gone by now. Even though Slocum didn't have a notion as to who'd pulled the trigger or where the shooter had been, there was no reason to tell Bensonn as much. "What happened?" Slocum growled. "You pushed your luck too damn far, you arrogant piece of shit. You think you could just stand there and talk me to death?"

Rob's eyes snapped around to look in every direction as if they were rattling in their sockets. "No. There was supposed to be . . . more."

"Yeah," Slocum said. "Lots of men in your spot think the same thing. You're riding with Abernathy?" When he didn't get a response right away, Slocum lowered himself to one knee, grabbed Bensonn by the front of his shirt, and lifted his upper body an inch or two off the ground. "What was the purpose of shooting up that saloon? Talk to me!"

"Why the . . . fuck would I talk to . . . you?"

"Because you don't have much time on this earth to talk to anyone else. Besides that, it ain't as if the men you thought would back you up are going to show their faces anytime soon." The look on Bensonn's face was more than enough to let Slocum know he'd touched a nerve. "That's right. I know you were expecting backup. The only other reason you'd stand there and lure me into one spot without taking any steps to defend yourself was if you were a damn fool who don't mind dying. I can tell by the terror in your eyes that isn't true."

"Go to hell."

"Not before you, asshole. And you'll be seeing the devil's face long before the men who left you swinging in the breeze are made to answer for what they've done. You want to have some measure of payback? Tell me where I can find your good-for-nothing partners."

Anger flashed across Rob's face, and he tried in vain to lift his Winchester. When he couldn't, his muscles slackened as if his entire body had suddenly given up its fight to survive. "Son of a bitch."

"You forced me into this, Rob."

"Not you!" he snapped. "Abernathy and that other one."

"What other one?"

"Justin."

Slocum could feel the bite on his fishing line but didn't want to pull too hard out of fear that he might lose his catch. Rather than press Rob further, he stood quietly and let the wounded man talk at his own pace.

"That . . . arrogant prick," Bensonn spat. "He was supposed to be here. I bet he . . . didn't even want to . . . to cut me loose from that jail cell."

"Who's Justin?" Slocum asked as a tentative prod to keep the conversation headed in the right direction.

"We were supposed to be . . . working together. Working to . . ."

Slocum recognized the light fading from Rob's eyes and hunkered down to get closer to him as he spoke in a louder, clearer voice. "You were left here to die, Rob. Anyone looking out for you could have filled me full of lead five times by now. Abernathy was the one to bust you out of Tarnish Mills?"

Rob nodded, which obviously caused him no small amount of pain.

"Then I want to hunt him down," Slocum said. "I'll make him answer for what he did."

Fighting to keep his eyes open, Rob glared up at him and said, "You don't give a shit about me dyin'. You don't give . . . a shit about anyone killin' me."

"You're right. I don't care about making him answer for killing you. I mean to make him regret killing the lawman who locked you up. From where you are right now, though, does it make a difference?" After that had soaked in for a second or two, Slocum added, "I aim to bring Abernathy to justice. Do you think he'll come along quietly?"

"Hell no!"

"And what about this Justin who's riding with him? Do you think—"

That question didn't even need to be fully formed before Bensonn laughed at it. "Justin would kill his own mama if he thought he could profit from it."

"There you go. Dead is dead. As long as them other two get put into the ground, what the hell difference does it make why they got there?"

Rob started to talk, but winced and arched his back as a wave of pain shot through him. Blood soaked into his shirt from the wound in his chest to form a spreading crimson pattern in the material. Seeing that, Slocum was reminded of the wound that had ushered Sheriff Cass from this world and into the next.

"They're . . . going to Hollister," Rob finally said.

"Directly from here?"

"Should be. That's where . . . I was . . . supposed to meet . . ."

As he watched the other man squirm, Slocum was tempted to fire one more bullet into the poor bastard just to put an end to him. It was the same courtesy he'd show to a wounded dog, which didn't seem fitting for someone like

Rob Bensonn. Any choice to be made on the matter was rendered pointless since Rob gave up his ghost with one last shudder that could be heard as his heel knocked against the ground.

Slocum scooped up the Winchester and continued running along the path he'd chosen when he'd first dashed down that alley. Folks were moving here and there as they made their way down winding paths that cut through the little settlement. There were no more gunshots fired and no more familiar voices raised to catch his attention. It was as if Spencer Flats had simply opened its mouth and swallowed Abernathy whole.

A few seconds later, Haresh wandered into Slocum's line of sight. The bigger man held his gaze and shrugged.

Since Haresh hadn't had any better luck, Slocum was left with two choices. He could either continue scouring the settlement by looking under every tent flap and through every crooked doorway. or he could turn around and head back to the saloon.

For the time being, Slocum gave in to the need for a stiff drink.

9

As Slocum approached Jocelyn's, he was stopped by Haresh. "I wouldn't advise anyone getting between me and another one of them beers," Slocum warned. "Could prove fatal."

The big man didn't budge. "Saloon's closed."

"Why? Hasn't the place ever gotten shot up before? Not much of a saloon if that's the case."

"Jocelyn was hit."

The halfhearted grin Slocum had been wearing was brushed away in an instant. "How bad?"

"She's being tended now."

"Where?"

"At her home. You," Haresh said while pinning him in place using one massive hand, "should stay away from her."

"Those men weren't after me."

"Just to be certain, you'll stay away from her."

Slocum wanted to argue, but he didn't have any pressing business with the bartender and Haresh was only acting as a cautious friend. "Just tell me how bad it was."

The big man sighed, which sounded like a massive wind

flowing back and forth between them. "She was hit in the knee. Just below, actually. Looks like it was a ricochet or an accident. I don't think anyone was aiming for her."

"That's good to hear. What about the other man who confronted Abernathy? I saw the younger one come out here but lost track of the older fellow in all the commotion."

"He's dead," Haresh said with all the inflection of a slab of beef. "Shot through the head while we were jumping for cover."

"God damn it. Do you even know who they were?"

"Lawmen."

Slocum felt something roll through him like a set of clawed, iron fingers raking beneath his skin. "Why didn't you tell me that before?"

"Because we didn't know you. You came in asking about strangers and *you're* the stranger to us. I don't know what the hell happened. All I know is I feel damned useless. I don't like feeling that way."

"Nobody does. Can I get a beer or not?"

"You won't bother Jocelyn?"

"No," Slocum replied. "Considering that I nearly got shot a few times myself, I'd say I'm entitled to at least get a look at her."

Reluctantly, the big man nodded.

Inside, the saloon was a mess. Not as bad as it had been a few minutes ago, but a mess all the same. The tables had been set upright although a few of them had been shot up so badly they would need to be replaced. Both of the South-ards lay on the floor. They'd been positioned side by side covered mostly by a tablecloth. Jocelyn was seated on the bar with her feet dangling over the side. A thin man tended to her leg and was already wrapping it in bandages. Slocum took that as a good sign.

"What are you smiling at?" she asked.

"Glad to see you're still with us. How are you feeling?"

Jocelyn patted the shoulder of the man in front of her.

"This one was a medic. Judging by the way he handles my leg, I'd say he's more used to dealing with corpses."

"You can fix yourself up, you know," the medic said.

She ignored that and looked to Slocum. "I thought you just came in for a beer." Nodding toward the front of the place, she added, "Mighty thin walls, you know."

"Then you'll also know Haresh is doing a good job watching out for your interests."

"That's what I pay him for." Fixing her eyes upon the partially covered bodies, she asked, "Will you be tracking down the men who did this?"

"Yes."

"Then I'll also pay Haresh to go with you."

"Why would you do something like that?" Slocum asked.

"Why would you do what you've been doing?"

Rather than go into lengthy explanations, Slocum reached into a pocket and produced the dented little deputy's badge.

"Are you new to this territory?" Jocelyn asked.

"No."

"Then you should know that the law is enforced differently around here than it is for states back East. We have to watch each other's backs, and when you get someone who thinks they can stroll into a peaceful town and shoot it up like a madman, then you've got to convince them otherwise."

"These parts are known for vigilantes," Slocum said.

"I'm no vigilante. I'm a concerned citizen and so is Haresh. If he would like to accompany you in finding the man who killed those two in cold blood in my place of business, then I'll be more than happy to pay for his expenses. It's your prerogative to refuse our help, but I don't see any good reason why you would do such a thing."

After taking a moment, Slocum said, "I can only think of one good reason."

Haresh stepped up to him and asked, "What is that?"

"I've already seen too many men die this week. I don't want to have your name added to that list."

"You won't."

"Ever fire a gun other than that cannon of a shotgun you use to frighten drunks?"

"Yes," Haresh replied without hesitation.

"At a man?"

The big fellow's eyes took on the intensity of coals that had been left at the bottom of a campfire for three days straight. "Yes," he growled.

"Killed a man?"

"What's this got to do with anything?" Jocelyn snapped. When she tried to scoot off the bar, she was held in place by the slender man who was almost finished tending to her wound. Leaning to one side so she could look around the medic, Jocelyn said, "Haresh will help you. Do you want his help or not?"

Shifting his attention fully to the bigger man, Slocum spoke as if they were the only ones inside the saloon. "I've never crossed paths with Abernathy before, but I've seen him shoot. He's damned fast and accurate to boot. He's also got an ace or two up his sleeve, which makes him even more dangerous. I'm going after him because I ain't about to be frightened off. If we get a chance to take a shot at a killer like him, we'll need to take it. No hesitation. No second thoughts. You pause one second to think about sending a man to meet his maker and that same man will burn a hole through you. Do you understand me?"

"Yes," Haresh replied. The intensity was still in his voice, but without the menace.

"So answer my question. Have you ever killed a man?"

Slocum had asked plenty of men that same question. More often than not, the words spoken in the response never told him as much as how they were said. Those with something to prove, usually younger men or kids, would pipe up right away with some kind of boast or bloody story about a fight to the death. Usually, that was all those were. Stories. Some men tried to shake off the question without saying much. Others would get angry as a way to deflect the whole thing. Haresh stared at Slocum with cold detachment before telling him, "I can help you. That's all you need to know."

There was something else going on behind the bigger man's eyes. Something haunted him, which was more than enough to answer Slocum's question. "All right, then," he said. "You can come along. Just do what I tell you and try not to get in my way."

When Haresh looked over at Jocelyn, it was like a dog asking for permission from its master to rip someone's throat out.

"You two try to get along," she said. "I'd rather not have killers like this Abernathy fellow roaming free. Bad for business. Mr. Slocum, I appreciate what you're doing and will help any way I can. Haresh . . ." What she said after that was in another language. Slocum thought it sounded like something from the Far East, but it wasn't Chinese. Before he could deduce any more than that, she'd stopped talking and was getting a reluctant nod from Haresh.

"Now," she said as the medic walked away to help himself to one of the bottles behind the bar, "if you'll excuse me, I have a business to run. You men can either get about your hunt or roll up your sleeves and start straightening up my saloon."

Judging by how quickly Haresh turned and stomped out the door, he'd had his fill of sweeping that floor and picking up those chairs.

Slocum followed him out. "I aim to get going as quickly as possible," he said to the big man's back. "We've already given Abernathy a head start, so—"

"He's still in town."

"What?"

Haresh stopped and turned around so quickly that Slocum almost ran into him. "I said he's still in town."

"Do you know that for certain?"

"No, but you should probably ride out and have a look for yourself just to be sure he didn't make camp nearby."

"Is that your way of getting rid of me?"

All it took was a sharp snap of his wrist for Haresh to point the shotgun up toward Slocum's chin. He'd carried the weapon so naturally that Slocum had forgotten the big man still had it. "If I wanted to get rid of you, I could think of a much easier way."

Slocum smirked and cocked his head. "Maybe not as easy as you might think." Then he directed Haresh's eyes down toward the Colt that had been drawn and aimed at the big man's gut. Apparently Slocum hadn't been the only one to underestimate someone's ability to use his weapon.

Haresh nodded and took a step back. "Perhaps we can get this job done together after all," he said while lowering the shotgun.

"I can do this job without you."

"And if Far Eye Abernathy thinks that's what you're doing, we will have an advantage, no?"

"Maybe." Slocum holstered the Colt. "Still think I should be the one to ride out and check the trails leaving town?"

"Yes. You were the one to charge after Abernathy and you were the one to shoot his partner, so you'll be the one he'd expect to charge after him on horseback. I'm just supposed to be a fixture at the saloon. Nobody takes much notice of me no matter what, so I can have a look around town without raising suspicion. Also, I'm guessing that I know this town better than you."

"You'd be guessing right. You still think I could catch sight of Abernathy after he's had this much time to ride off?"

Haresh nodded. "One trail leading from town is down a stretch of land that goes for miles bordered with trees on both sides that are too dense for a horse to get through. The other trail is on an open stretch of a rocky pass. Any man with working eyes could catch sight of another rider two or three miles away. That is, if he knows what to look for."

Although Slocum didn't like being the one sent off on an errand, he had to admit that Haresh's reasoning made sense.

"Fine," he grunted. "Since we've both wasted too much time, I'll ride out and see what I can see while you have a look around town. I take it you know where a man might hole up around here?"

"I make my living chasing scum from a saloon," he replied. "I know where a man might go to cool his heels and I know where he might go to find someone else to come after me once he sobers up. Now why don't you go and see if you can spot a man on horseback on a barren stretch of road from half a mile away?" With that, Haresh slapped Slocum on the shoulder and walked away. The gesture seemed friendly enough, but nearly knocked Slocum out of his boots.

Once Slocum climbed into his saddle, a sense of urgency washed through his blood to ignite it quicker than a match touched to a jug of kerosene. Having run plenty of gunmen out of plenty of towns, he knew that most of them tended to go in a straight line as quickly as they could. The ones that had a more intricate escape plan weren't about to be caught even without a head start anyway. So Slocum tapped his heels against his stallion's sides and followed the main street north out of Spencer Flats.

The town wasn't given such a name by chance. It was situated on a flat plane of rock surrounded by jagged hills and thick clusters of trees that came together to form a wooded area just as Haresh had described. If anyone was going to travel off that trail, it wouldn't be on horseback. Slocum rode for a ways before picking a spot and digging into his saddlebag for his field glasses. Having used that trail to enter town the first time, he knew it was more or less a straight shot. Gazing through the lenses of the glasses showed him only one horse-drawn cart that wouldn't get to town in under an hour. Other than that, the trail was clear.

Slocum brought his horse around, raced to town, slowed enough to keep from trampling anyone, and was soon charging down the other trail that led toward a low range of mountains. He didn't have to ride for long to see there was nobody on that trail. His view was so good that he wondered if Spencer Flats had started out as a military encampment. The positioning was perfect for keeping watch on any would-be invaders. Just to be certain, Slocum gazed through the field glasses once again. He found a few wildcats, but not much else.

When he rode back, the sun was on its way toward the western horizon. Thanks to all of the trees and mountains surrounding Spencer Flats, shadows crept across the shoddy town earlier than normal. Patches of darkness topped by slivers of brilliant orange and yellow sunlight gave the place a life of its own. Slocum tied his horse off in front of Jocelyn's, but didn't go into the saloon. Instead, he crossed the street and began walking. Along the way, he studied as many faces as he could, looking for someone who was either familiar or suspicious. As with most settlements that could be torn down or blown away by a stiff breeze, the latter wasn't hard to find.

Montana was a beautiful territory protected by men who had the will and firepower to do the job. Vigilantes terrorized some towns worse than known outlaws, providing a system that was strangely balanced. Much like the system used in nature, Montana rewarded the strong and punished the weak. Slocum not only respected it, but saw a rough beauty to it all.

That system was in motion wherever he looked, even if it was down the unimpressive streets of Spencer Flats. For every storekeeper or pleasant local who returned his gaze with a friendly smile, there were men and women who shot him a threatening glare or looked away as quickly as they could. Slocum expected a hotter reception from Abernathy or anyone riding with him. Stumbling upon one of them would mean having to defend himself in the blink of an eye.

After seeing Abernathy shoot, Slocum guessed he might not have any notice whatsoever before a bullet came for him. That wasn't such a bad thing. If there was nothing to be done about some terrible looming thing, a man could just sit back and let it happen.

Slocum's attention was so finely tuned that he saw the door to the boardinghouse directly in front of him start to open before the hinges began to creak. Then again, he would have had to be blind and deaf to miss the approach of the man who stepped outside once it was open.

"Back so soon?" Haresh asked as he shut the boardinghouse door behind him.

"There wasn't much to see. What about you? Anything interesting?"

"Possibly."

"If you're going to make me dig for every answer, our conversations are going to be pretty damn cumbersome."

"The woman who runs this place rented a room to Far Eye Abernathy."

"You described him to her?" Slocum asked.

"Didn't have to. He signed her register."

"As Far Eye Abernathy?"

Haresh grinned. "No. As F. Abernathy. Want to go see for yourself?"

Although he considered it, Slocum decided to give the man some slack until he proved unworthy of it. "What should we do next?"

"Wait here. He'll be back."

"You sure?"

"Yes. His things are still in the room."

Slocum studied Haresh's face before questioning him again. He may have only known the big man a short time, but there was nothing in his features to make Slocum think he was lying. "Where should we wait?"

"In the other room to rent. One of us can sit there as long

as we don't make a mess and I didn't have to sign the register."

"And the other keeps watch from somewhere else?"

"I thought that might be a good plan."

"So it is," Slocum said. "Perhaps we might be able to get this job done after all."

10

Slocum took first watch inside the boardinghouse. A few minutes after Haresh disappeared around a corner, Slocum verified the big man's story. The first part was easy enough to check. After introducing himself to the plump woman who owned the place, he was allowed to take a quick look at the register. Sure enough, *F. Abernathy* was scrawled right where it was supposed to be.

Next, he went upstairs to the room they were allowed to use. Everything was neat and tidy. So much so that Slocum felt bad about sitting in the small chair with the padded seat situated in a corner next to a window. Fortunately, he didn't intend on sitting very long. Although the woman who owned the place was friendly and had a wide, beaming smile, she was heavier than Slocum and walked with a slow, plodding waddle that bent the floorboards with every step. The house was one of the few permanent structures in town, but wasn't put together any better than the frame that held the roof of Jocelyn's saloon off the ground. When he heard the stout woman head into the kitchen, Slocum crossed the upstairs hallway and tested the knob to Abernathy's room.

The door was locked.

Slocum gnawed on the inside of one cheek while thinking about how he might get into that room. Actually, getting in wasn't such a big problem. Getting in without being kicked out or raising unneeded suspicion was where it got tricky. To solve that problem, he took a second to think about the house itself. All Slocum had to do was smell the musty air or listen to the dozens of creaks accompanying every movement within to know the house had been in town longer than most of its residents. He ran a finger along the doorframe, picking up a splinter for his trouble. That sharp sting brought a smile to his face.

He prodded the frame a bit harder and was almost able to pry away a sizable chunk of wood. Nodding to himself, Slocum grabbed the handle and placed one shoulder against the door. He waited for the next series of creaks before leaning his weight against it and pushing until some more of the wood gave way. It took less effort than he'd anticipated, meaning the house was even older than he'd thought. Either that, or this wasn't the first time the door had been forced open. Considering some of the things that Haresh had told him about the type of men that came through Spencer Flats, he figured the latter could have been just as likely as the former.

Whatever the reason, the door came open with a subtle crunch and Slocum was glad for it. He stepped inside with one hand resting upon the Colt at his hip. The room was a little messy, but not dangerous. Slocum kept his hand on his gun as he walked around the room, peeking under the bed and into a narrow closet.

A carpetbag sat on the floor at the foot of the bed. It was halfway full with neatly folded clothes. A waistcoat lay across the back of a chair. When Slocum picked it up to see if it could have fit Abernathy, he found a holster made from expensive, perfectly maintained leather. The gun inside was a pearl-handled .32. Small enough to be concealed and large enough to get the job done. Suddenly, the house creaked and something scraped against the wall from the outside.

Freezing in place, Slocum shifted his eyes to the window. Since there was no movement outside and he was pretty sure there was no balcony out there, he wondered if sound echoed differently in that room than it had in the hall. Leaning toward the door, he listened for any hint that the owner of the place could be on her way to check on him. After a few seconds, he heard her singing to herself as she continued to shuffle noisily in the kitchen.

He also heard another, louder scrape against the wall.

As Slocum turned back around, the window was lifted up an inch or two by a set of pale, bony fingers. Rather than approach the window, Slocum took a quiet step back and eased his Colt from its holster.

The fingers wrapped around the edge of the sill, grabbed it tightly, and whitened as a strained grunt came from outside. Soon, another set of fingers slid over the sill and the top of a hat began to rise above the lower edge of the window.

Even though he was seeing someone pull himself up the side of the house, Slocum was having a hard time believing it. Mainly, he was impressed by how quiet the other man was being. Sure, he'd heard enough to catch his attention, but the floor creaked every time he shifted his weight and the walls groaned whenever a bird flew too damn close. Having someone scale the wall without making enough ruckus to raise the dead was one hell of a feat.

The hat came up a bit more until a set of narrowed eyes made it over the top of the sill. When they focused on him, Slocum smirked at the eyes and gave an offhanded wave.

"Evenin'," he said.

With a strained groan, the man outside let go with one set of fingers. Before he could drop out of sight, Slocum rushed forward to get a look at who'd made the ascent. Whoever the man was, his intention wasn't to let go and drop back to street level. When Slocum took a look down at the man, he found himself gazing into the wrong end of a pistol barrel.

"Jesus!" Slocum grunted as he threw himself back and away from the window.

The gun barked once, blasting a chunk from the sill and drilling a hole into the ceiling.

"Are you shooting up there?" the woman asked from downstairs.

Slocum wasn't about to waste his breath answering her question. He aimed his Colt from the hip, squeezed its trigger, and made a hole of his own. The pistol's round drilled through the wall directly beneath the sill, sending a plume of dust into the air inside and out.

Since the first set of fingers was no longer wrapped around the sill, Slocum moved forward to get a look outside. Every instinct he possessed screamed for him to steer clear of that window. The moment he tried to look through it, a series of gunshots were fired up at him from ground level.

Slocum charged through the room while replacing spent cartridges from his pistol with fresh ones from his gun belt. He kicked open the door and took a few steps, only to be blocked by a very large, very angry, woman.

"What is the meaning of this?" the house's owner asked. Seemingly unmoved by the gunfire, she had her hands placed on her hips and a stern expression on her face.

"Step aside, ma'am."

"I've dealt with all sorts of men and I refuse to be—"

She may have been a big woman, but she wasn't too big for Slocum to physically move aside so he could get by. She sputtered and protested, but in the end, she was shouting her protests to Slocum's back. As long as she didn't try to follow him, he was inclined to leave her be.

Slocum raced outside. Before he could get around to get to the side of the house where the broken window could be found, he heard the crackle of more gunshots erupting in the distance. All he could see was the flash of sparks erupting from gun barrels about a hundred yards away.

He took a direct path toward the fight. In a matter of seconds the gunshots dwindled away, leaving only the shouts of people who'd found themselves too close to the commotion. Slocum could see one figure standing tall with a gun in his hand. Recognizing that figure as Haresh, he approached and announced his presence so as not to surprise the big man.

"Don't shoot," Slocum said. "It's me."

"That man is a snake," Haresh growled. "He slithered past me and all the men I had looking out for him."

"How many men are we talking about?"

Haresh remained focused on the street in front of him. Although there was plenty of movement to be found, all of it came from locals who rushed about like bits of dirt that had been kicked up to swirl in a bucket of water. "Just some customers who don't mind alerting me when they see someone walking down a particular alley. I asked some of them to shout or fire a shot in the air if they saw anyone approaching that house. Stupid," he sighed. "That snake got past me, so it's no surprise he got past a bunch of drunks who were probably distracted by a card game or lack of sleep."

"Well, he got past me, too. Twice. Son of a bitch. I don't think it was Abernathy, though. That was no old man climbing up the side of that building. Maybe calling him a spider is more fitting than a snake."

Haresh turned an angry face toward Slocum. "You are in high spirits after losing that man."

"Nothing to be done about it now," Slocum said with a shrug. "We've already tried chasing one of them through this town without any luck. And that was the older one, mind you. They've got this place scouted out pretty well, and wherever those men are right now, it's safe to say they're dug in worse than a tick."

"So you want to give up?"

"Not hardly. I'm just saying we'd be wasting our time running around this town like a couple of idiots. Last time, one of them laid a trap. I was fortunate enough to get out of it alive, but I ain't about to push my luck by floundering around a second time."

"Then we go back to the boardinghouse," Haresh said.

Slocum watched the bigger man carefully as he asked, "And why would you do that?"

"Because whatever's there was important enough for one of them to sneak back and get it."

Nodding sagely, Slocum slapped Haresh on the back. "I might make something of a tracker out of you yet."

When Slocum returned to the boardinghouse, he truly was in fairly high spirits. Haresh had been thinking along the same lines as he had, which meant working with him might actually be a boon instead of a chore. Not only that, but Haresh stepped right up to the woman who owned the boardinghouse like a man placing himself between his friend and the business end of a cannon. She exploded as soon as they walked through the door, but Slocum was able to sneak upstairs while Haresh continued to apologize and accept the brunt of her complaints.

Upstairs, there wasn't much to see. The room was just as it had been when Slocum had broken in just a little while ago. Since he could hear the woman downstairs was still busy putting Haresh through the wringer, he took some time to look under the bed, behind the dresser, and in every corner before sifting through the contents of the carpetbag.

Even when Haresh's voice became the predominant one in the conversation and the woman's heavy steps pounded up the stairs, Slocum continued to look for something worthy of all the effort that had been expended that night.

She stomped down the hall and pushed open the door as Slocum was running his hands along the bottom of the carpetbag. "This whole thing is highly . . . wait a second," she gasped. "What happened to my door?"

Slocum looked up to see the house's owner leaning forward to examine the part of the frame that had been splintered and broken when he'd pushed through to gain entrance to the room. Haresh appeared behind her in the hall and sputtered, "Whatever it is, I'm sure we can—"

"The man who started all the shooting did it," Slocum said.

The woman rubbed the broken doorframe as if it were a baby with a busted arm. "What?"

"The one who came in here," Slocum explained. "I thought I heard something strange, so I stepped out of my room. Then this young fella smashed the door open so I chased him out. He jumped through the window and got away."

It was a flimsy story to say the least, but Slocum stood behind it as if it were gospel. "Why would anyone do such a thing?" she asked.

Slocum placed his hands on his hips and sighed. "That's what I was in here trying to figure out, ma'am. All I can tell you for certain is that the man who rented this room from you wasn't what he appeared to be. That is, of course, going under the assumption that you don't cater to gunmen or thieves."

"I don't know what anyone does in their own time, but I assure you I am a proper Christian woman!"

"That's what I figured. And since I'm partially responsible for this mess," Slocum continued, "it's only proper if I help pay for the damages." He dug into his pocket and produced a few silver dollars. "Will this suffice?"

She approached him and touched the coins tentatively. "Actually, I know some people around town that would help me fix this up."

Slocum turned her hand palm-up and placed the coins there. "Then use this for supplies or just as a way for us to say thank you for putting up with all the noise."

"Well . . . that's right kind of you." She stuck the coins into a pocket sewn into her skirts and smiled graciously. "I suppose since you were under my care, I should be partially responsible for what happened here."

"Don't be ridiculous, ma'am."

"If there's anything I can do to help . . ."

"What will you be doing with this man's things?" Haresh asked while sweeping out one arm to encompass the carpetbag and most of the rest of the room.

"I'll be holding on to them until the proper owner returns, I guess," she replied.

"Will you allow us to take them to him?"

"You'd do that?"

Slocum flashed the deputy badge he'd been given as if it granted him the rights and privileges of the president himself. "We'll be looking for him in connection to what happened here, so it's my duty to return these items as well. No need for a fine, upstanding citizen like yourself to be troubled any further."

Responding more to the smooth tone in Slocum's voice instead of the words themselves, the woman flushed slightly in the cheeks and smiled sheepishly. "I'm not one to stand in the way of a lawman. Especially one as fine . . . I mean . . . respectable as yourself."

Slocum gave her a prize-winning smile and tipped his hat. "Much appreciated, ma'am."

Haresh remained silent until the woman walked past him and went back downstairs. Finally, he stepped farther into the room to help Slocum gather up Abernathy's belongings. "That was quite a show," he muttered.

"I thought so."

"Why lie to her? If you were going to pay her for the damages, you could have just told her what happened."

"I doubt she'd be so friendly if she knew I busted her door before knowing there was anything at all going on in here. Besides, I know you might come back to this town and

deal with these folks. I thought it would serve you better if
you remained on good terms with people like her instead
of becoming known for associating with people like me."

"People like you, eh? I'm starting to get a much better
idea of what that means."

The two of them cleaned out the room without wasting
a second. They may have been on good terms with the
owner, but they both knew better than to expect that to last
forever. In fact, Slocum even went back into the room he'd
been allowed to use and made sure everything was good
and tidy. On their way out, they said respectful farewells to
the woman and slipped out through the front door.

Their horses were tied out front and Slocum climbed into
his saddle as soon as he'd freed the reins.

"What are you doing?" Haresh asked.

"Leaving. Aren't you coming with me?"

"Yes, but it won't be long before it's too dark to ride."

"I've gotten a look at the trails leading away from here,"
Slocum said. "They're not bad. Besides, this isn't the first
time I've been through this territory."

"What about Abernathy?"

"I think I know where he's headed."

Haresh reached up to grab the horn of Slocum's saddle,
effectively stopping the horse in its tracks. "We don't even
know if he's in town, camping somewhere, or if he intends
to leave."

"We're not doing a damn bit of good trying to catch him
and his men here. Each time one of them slips away from
us, they'll only be more slippery the next time around.
Besides, if they meant to clean out that room, odds are they
wanted to pull up stakes and get out of town."

"Are you certain of that?"

"No," Slocum said. "It's a hunch. A damn powerful one.
And like I already said, I think I know where they're
headed."

"How do you know this?"

Slocum pulled on his reins, causing the stallion to turn away from Haresh. Although the big man could have put up more of a struggle, he allowed the horn to slip from his grasp. "Abernathy is working with that man who tried to get into his room. It's just too big of a coincidence to think he was some random thief climbing up there and shooting at me when he was spotted. One of their men was already killed in this town, and they'll know better than to take another run at reclaiming whatever the hell they were after tonight. Figuring they'll stay here after all of that is figuring Abernathy and this other fellow are idiots."

"They may be snakes," Haresh said, "but they are not fools."

"Exactly. While I don't know exactly what's running through their heads, I know it's high time for them to cut and run. Since I have an idea of where they're going, I'm setting out now. Whether I make it a few miles or halfway tonight, it's a hell of a lot better than sitting here and kicking my feet up while Abernathy gets even more of a jump on us."

11

As Haresh had predicted, they didn't make it very far that night before needing to find a spot to camp. They may have made it a bit farther if they hadn't stopped to load up on supplies, but they wouldn't have had much of a camp without them. Even considering the short detour, they managed to put a few miles between them and Spencer Flats before choosing to call it quits for the night.

Slocum built a fire that was just large enough to provide a touch of warmth while keeping some animals away, and Haresh opened a can of beans for each of them. "So," the big man said while scooping some of the mushy beans into his mouth, "what are your aces?"

"What?"

"Before, you mentioned having some aces up your sleeve. What are they?"

"One of them was the conversation I had with that man I found after Jocelyn's place was shot up."

"You mean the man you killed?"

"That's right," Slocum replied. "It took some convincing,

but I got him to talk. One of the things he told me was that he was supposed to meet Abernathy in Hollister."

Haresh squinted at the fire. "I think I've heard of that place."

"Yeah? Well, I'd hope so, considering you work in a saloon. I've even heard of it. Hollister made a name for itself in the last year or two as being a stop on the gamblers' circuit. It was a little mining camp before then, and after the card players set their sights on the place, the town went through something of a boom."

"Card players can make a town grow?"

Slocum dug into his beans with a dented old spoon. "I don't mean to say the town became some huge success on account of poker, but it went from a camp to . . . well . . . a bigger camp because of all the folks that took notice of the place. I'm sure there's other factors at play, but it's growing slowly and surely. It's also a place where outlaws can hang their hats with relative comfort. Vigilantes aren't welcome there and neither is the law."

"Sounds savage," Haresh said with distaste showing plainly upon his face.

"Folks look out for themselves around here. They like it that way and it works out pretty well for them. As for being savage, I'd say you've got just as much chance getting shot or robbed in Hollister as you would in places like New York City or Tombstone."

Haresh's eyes widened, and a very rare smile made an appearance on his dark, weathered face. "You have been to New York City?"

"I have. The difference between there and Hollister is that men who step out of line in Hollister know they'll have to answer to someone for it. It may appear savage on the surface, but there's a certain elegance that comes along with such a simple system working so perfectly."

"Nature has a system like that as well. Kill or be killed. That does not make it civilized."

"See, there's your mistake," Slocum pointed out. "I never said any of these towns were civilized."

"So Abernathy is going to Hollister. That is the only ace you had up your sleeve?"

"Nope. That dying gunman also named another one of Abernathy's accomplices. Justin."

"Justin? That is all?"

Now that he'd all but cleaned out the can of beans in his hand, Slocum rattled his spoon along the bottom to make sure he'd gotten every last bite. "That's all. Sound familiar?"

"If you're asking if I've ever heard of someone named Justin, then yes."

"That's not what I mean. Have you ever heard of someone who might be riding with a killer like Abernathy? An outlaw. A known man in these parts. Someone like that . . . named Justin?"

Setting down his empty can, Haresh grunted, "No."

"Well, at least we have a name to give to folks when we get to Hollister and start asking around. Could spark someone's memory. If we get lucky, we might even run into someone who's looking for someone with that name as well."

"There really is no rhyme or reason to what you're doing, is there?" Haresh asked.

"Of course there is. You just can't see it yet."

"And neither can you." The big man grinned. "Still, there is some bravery to be found in a man who walks into a cave without knowing how many bears he will have to wrestle."

"That a fancy way for saying I'm fat, dumb, and happy?"

After thinking it over for a second, Haresh nodded. "I suppose so. My way sounded better."

"So it did. I got something else from our little run-in with Abernathy, though. Something that no dying man had to tell me."

Haresh had busied himself with his bedroll, and once

he'd spread it out reasonably close to the fire, he asked, "Are you going to tell me or do I need to praise you for your observational skills?"

"Back at that saloon, Abernathy didn't take all those shots on his own."

"That is no surprise. We have already found at least two partners riding with him."

"That's not what I mean," Slocum said. "I'm talking about the actual shots he fired during that commotion. When I went back to examine some of the damage done, I could tell that some of them bullet holes were made by a rifle."

Haresh scowled at him and asked, "How could you tell that just by looking?"

"I've been fired at more times than I can count. I've had to track more men than I can remember. In all that time, I've picked up a thing or two. One of them is being able to tell the difference between shots that came from a pistol and a rifle. Kind of how a trapper can tell the difference between wolf and dog prints. Granted, it was just a suspicion I had before, but it panned out when I put more of the pieces together."

Although he tried to cover it with a disapproving stare, Haresh's interest was clearly sparked. "Like what?"

"Like how Abernathy could fire a shot at me outside of that saloon with a pistol from over seventy yards away and send a bullet whipping past my head?"

"He is a good shot."

"He'd also have to be a groundbreaking gunsmith because the effective range of those .44s he carried is about fifty yards. Even if his gun could cover that distance, there's no chance in hell he could get so close to hitting me while on the run." Seeing the question start to form behind Haresh's eyes, Slocum added, "*No* chance."

"So what are you proposing?"

"I'm proposing that he's cheating. It's not a terribly complex scheme. All he does is stand up front and bluster loud enough to draw every eye to him. When he starts to fire, he's got an accomplice with a rifle somewhere behind him firing at his targets. It's just a deadlier spin on an old magician's technique."

"How would the accomplice know all of his targets?" Haresh asked. "They could have the first one worked out ahead of time, but what happens when things get wild?"

"He starts firing away and his accomplice covers him. You were there when he shot up Jocelyn's place. Can you honestly tell me you know his guns were pointed at the spot where every bullet was delivered?"

"No. We were all firing a lot of shots."

"Which is exactly how that scheme can work."

"But what about when a man is fighting one on one?" Haresh asked. "Far Eye Abernathy earned his reputation by gunning men down in street fights and killing gunmen on his own. There were witnesses. Surely he couldn't have cheated all those times without being noticed."

"I'm not saying he cheated every time," Slocum replied. "I'm saying he cheated at Jocelyn's saloon and that he's probably cheated on other occasions as well. Mix in that system of his with some genuine skill and you've got a man to be reckoned with who's building up a reputation that's good enough to be head of his own gang."

"This means we can't go after him like we would a normal outlaw. Without knowing who we are dealing with, how many there are, and where they are aiming, we would be fighting in the dark at all times. I have not hunted many men," Haresh told him in a strained voice that showed how much of an effort it was to admit ignorance in the matter. "This one is more dangerous than I thought. Perhaps you were right in the first place. Perhaps I will be more of a burden than a help in this matter."

"I wouldn't go so far as all that," Slocum said. "In fact, a wild card may be just what we need to tip the balances.

The hardest part when dealing with a trickster is in figuring out you're being tricked."

"Like the magician you talked about. Many of those illusions rely on a willing audience."

"Yep. And now that we know we're being tricked, we're not a very willing audience. The next step is to try and figure out how to break this magician's illusions down to their separate parts. In this case, those parts are the accomplices he's got covering him when he goes into a place to shoot it full of holes."

"What will he be doing in Hollister?" Haresh asked.

"All that dying man told me was that he was supposed to meet up with Abernathy there."

"If that accomplice was killed, who's to say he wasn't given bad information in the first place?"

Slocum thought back to the surprised look on Rob's face when he'd been shot and the anger in his voice soon after. Those were the expressions of a man who didn't even know there was a possibility of being stabbed in the back when the blade slid into him. What Slocum had to decide now was whether that was the look of a man who'd been double-crossed on a whim after being a trusted member of Abernathy's gang or if he was a loose end that had been trimmed after being strung along by men he'd mistaken as friends.

"I'll be honest," Slocum said. "There's no way for me to tell you we can fully believe what Bensonn told me. All I can say is that he believed he was supposed to meet up with his partners in Hollister. I looked into his eyes as he died, and there ain't much room for lying at that moment."

Haresh was lying on his back, looking up at the stars, as he nodded solemnly. His gaze was so intense that it seemed to pierce the velvety black sky when he said, "I have seen eyes like that as well. It takes a powerful resolve to speak lies when a man is so close to seeing his god."

"I may not have known Rob Bensonn for long, but he

didn't strike me as a man with anything close to powerful resolve."

"Then he believed he was to go to Hollister."

"Yes." Suddenly something hit Slocum like a bolt of lightning. "And just maybe whoever shot him wanted to do him in before he could spill that fact to anyone else."

In the next several moments, the only sounds to be heard were the crackling of the fire and the rustling of critters in the nearby trees. Finally Haresh said, "That is an awfully large maybe."

"Yes, it is," Slocum admitted. "But it's all we got."

12

Ferril Abernathy's camp was similar to Slocum's in one respect: there was a fire. Despite having been set up in a similar amount of time and under hectic circumstances while trying to avoid being spotted from afar, Abernathy still managed to erect a small tent and find enough time to groom himself. The scents hanging in the air were all that remained of a supper he'd prepared consisting of fried pork loin and greens sautéed in lard. The man himself sat upon a small stool that could be folded up and stored in one of two large packs carried by a horse that had lost its rider.

Compared to the distinguished gentleman who sat upon his stool pruning a narrow strip of chin whiskers with a small set of scissors, the man who paced on the other side of the fire looked like something that had crawled in from the mountains. He was short in stature and narrow of build. The dirt covering his face was more of a thick crust that would require a chisel to remove. A thick coat of whiskers sprouted from his skin and his squint was so severe that it was impossible to determine the color of his eyes. They were simply dark, as was his mood.

"How can you sit there primping like a goddamn woman?" the skinny man asked.

Abernathy lifted his chin and screwed up his face in an expression meant to grant him cleaner access to the whiskers closest to his Adam's apple. "Contrary to what you may believe, women are not the only ones who need to take care of themselves. Appearances mean a lot, you know."

"Yeah. I *do* know. Mostly on account of me bein' the one who gives you them appearances!"

"Keep your voice down, Justin. No need to share our conversation with every living thing residing in these mountains."

"If I want to converse with you, I can do it any damn way I please."

Although Abernathy's movements were subtle, there was no mistaking the power behind them. When he turned to look directly at Justin, he did so using precise, perfectly refined muscle control that didn't force him to move the scissors away from his throat. He even clipped the next few whiskers without using the small round mirror in his hand. "Are you unhappy with our arrangement?"

"Finally picked up on that, did you?"

"Your hints were quite exaggerated." Setting down the mirror and picking up a small leather case, Abernathy said, "All right, then. Tell me what's on your mind."

"I think Slocum may have had a word or two with Rob before he died."

"That's funny. How could Rob survive more than a few moments with you gunning for him? After all, you've been so anxious to shoot everything full of holes no matter where we go anymore."

"You don't like the way I work?" Justin snapped. "Then maybe you should do yer own shooting from now on."

Abernathy placed his scissors into their leather case and set it down as if there was a spot for the case outlined in the dirt near his feet. Then he stood up, straightened his vest with a quick tug, and worked a kink out of his neck by twisting his head to one side. "If you have so little confidence in my shooting, then perhaps you'd like to put me to the test?"

Justin's face twitched and his body froze. "I just don't think you know enough about this Slocum fella."

"I've heard the name and I've heard a thing or two in regards to the man's reputation."

"Then you should know he ain't the sort that should be trifled with."

"That wasn't my intention," Abernathy said in a voice that was haughty and elegant without resorting to something as simple as an accent. Even without such an affectation, his words sounded as crisp and clean as polished silver.

"Well, he's mixed up in this now," Justin said. "In fact, he's probably out there closing in on us while you sit there staring into that mirror."

"You had an opportunity to shoot him in Spencer Flats. In fact, I might venture to say he's one of the few things in that saloon you *didn't* shoot."

"I did what I was supposed to do," Justin growled. "Keeping your sorry ass from being killed is work enough."

"If you would have done what I'd asked and merely killed the younger deputy at that table, we wouldn't be in this predicament. Now we'll have to find another lead in regards to the California job, and to make matters worse, you've drawn the ire of someone like John Slocum."

"Yeah? Well, maybe I wouldn't have had to draw no ire if you hadn't made me go back into town to fetch your damn clothes!"

"A job, I might add, that you failed to do since I am out several shirts, a pair of silk trousers, and one fine pair of shoes. I suppose I'll just tack that expense onto the ever-growing list of your shortcomings."

Justin was beyond words by now. His eyes opened and closed in a set of nervous blinks before his hand went for the old pistol strapped to his side. Although his speed would have been adequate under most circumstances, it wasn't enough to beat Abernathy to the punch. The well-dressed older man took one of his .44s from its holster and pointed its barrel at Justin in a smooth set of motions that had taken a lifetime to perfect.

"I appreciate you being upset," Abernathy said as he coolly thumbed back the .44's hammer. "But do you want your final mistake to be this one?"

"I ain't no idiot," Justin said.

"I never called you one."

"Well, that's what you meant."

One of Abernathy's eyebrows slid upward in a perfectly straight vertical line. "Perhaps that is what I implied. For that, you have my apologies."

"All right, then," Justin said as he stared at the older man's unwavering gun hand. His brow trembled and both corners of his mouth twitched as he figured as many of the angles as he could. In the end, the situation was all too simple. If he thought he could get an accurate shot off quicker than Abernathy, he could take it. If not, he had to holster his gun. When he holstered his gun, Justin tried his hardest to make it seem as if he was doing the older man a favor.

Abernathy accepted the gesture gracefully. "There's no need to fight," he said while placing his .44 into its proper place. "I thought going into town for my things would be an easy matter for someone of your talents." Before that could be interpreted as a slight, Abernathy added, "Obviously, neither one of us figured Slocum would be on our trail so quickly. Or at all, for that matter."

"What the hell does he want with us anyhow? You think he knew anyone we shot?"

"Several of the things I heard about him involved riding in a posse or helping a lawman in some other fashion. Perhaps I was correct in assuming it would be a mistake to kill that sheriff."

"There wasn't no choice. We had to break Rob out."

"I had the situation well in hand. That lawman wasn't anxious to draw his gun and there wasn't any help on its way. We could have removed Rob from that jail without it becoming such a messy affair."

"That lawman went for his gun," Justin said.

"I don't think so."

"Well, your eyes ain't what they used to be, are they? That's why you've got me and Rob along to do our part."

"Now . . . just you."

Justin grinned at that. "You got that right. And since it's just you and me, we gotta stick together more than ever."

Abernathy nodded as he lowered himself onto his stool. When he let out a breath, it was as if a heavy burden had dropped onto his shoulders. "There's only one more job ahead of us. We've come a long way to get here and we've almost got all of the pieces to get it done. That man you say you know . . . the one who has a touch with safes . . . he's supposed to be in Hollister?"

"That's right. If he ain't, I know how we can find him."

"He was supposed to be in Spencer Flats," Abernathy said in a voice that had grown tight as a bowstring. "And Tarnish Mills before that."

"A man like him has to move around a lot," Justin replied with a shrug. "What the hell am I supposed to do about it?"

"So far, everything we've had to acquire for this job has been moved around a lot. The informants who knew where to find the gold, the clerks who would know when it was being delivered to California, the make and model of the safes, the layout of the bank and its guard schedule . . ."

"We need all of them things, don't we?"

"Yes," Abernathy sighed. "We do. I only wish we haven't had to spill so much blood along the way."

Justin sat down on the ground, stretched out his legs, rested his head upon the saddle lying on the perimeter of the fire's light, and crossed his arms over his chest. "You didn't think such valuable information would be unguarded, did you?"

"Of course not."

"And those men we needed to capture. Did you think they'd give up what they knew or what they had without bein' squeezed?"

"Now you're the one assuming I'm an idiot," Abernathy scowled.

"I'm just layin' it all out for you."

"*I'm* the one who brought you into this! I laid it all out for *you*! You and Rob and Pete."

Justin nodded quickly. "You sure did. This is your job, Far Eye. You're the one with the reputation that's allowed us to get this far. And even though Pete and Rob both got killed on this job of yours, I'm still with you."

Until a few moments ago, Abernathy's calm had been an unbreakable wall. Every primping of his whiskers, straightening of his suit, and polishing of his boots fortified that wall and kept him walking proudly through damn near everything. Jumping to his feet, Abernathy rested his left hand upon one of his holstered .44s and used his right to jab a finger at Justin. "That's right! This is *my* job and you're just along for the ride! You're not the one up front when the shots are fired! You're not the one putting your life on the line!"

"Rob was covering you when he was found and killed," Justin reminded him. "You ain't the only one sticking his neck out."

"Well, I'm the one with the price on his head, and every time one of these events turns sour, *I'm* the one that gets most of the blame. Do you have any idea how much trouble is stirred up when a lawman is gunned down? Do you have any notion of how badly other lawmen will want to make an example of me or avenge a colleague's death? And don't forget where you are! This is vigilante territory! Those men are animals out hunting for men like you and me the way red men hunt for scalps!"

"I don't believe I've ever seen you get so worked up about anything, Ferril."

The older man was on him in a flash, hunkering down to grab hold of Justin's shirt and lift him less than an inch off the ground. That's as far as he needed to go to meet the sharpened steel of the knife that Abernathy had pulled from where it had been hiding. The blade was about two inches long and shaped like a wedge. The handle fit around his two middle fingers and the blade extended between them as if it had sprung from the top of his fist.

"Let me tell you something, boy," Abernathy snarled. "You haven't seen how worked up I can get. Just because I'm using men like you and Rob doesn't mean I need you to get this job done. You're here to make things go smoother. Easier. Faster. Instead, I find myself in a bloody goddamn mess with dead lawmen piling up on all sides."

"Take it easy, Ferril!" Given a sharp jolt by the fist that held him, Justin felt the tip of the other man's blade poke through his shirt to jab into his chest. Some blood trickled beneath his clothing. "I . . . I mean Mr. Abernathy."

"It's about goddamn time you spoke to me with respect. Just because you've been with me for the longest on this ride doesn't grant you special privileges. Understand?"

"Yes."

"And just because you can carry a gun doesn't make you a dangerous man. You're a killer. I know that much for certain, but even that doesn't make you dangerous. Want to know what does?"

The knife hadn't dug any deeper into Justin's chest, but it was slowly twisting back and forth as if to milk the shallow flesh wound for every ounce of pain it could produce. The more it twisted, the less Justin could concentrate. Therefore, instead of saying anything in response to the question that had been posed, he simply nodded.

"A dangerous man kills someone up close, where he can look into his victim's eyes and listen to the poor soul beg for one last breath," Abernathy said. "He does this even though it haunts him, and when the time comes, he does it again. A dangerous man knows he's damned for what he's done and isn't afraid to keep doing more. He knows he won't have to answer to any Good Lord when he's finally brought down in what will most certainly be an ugly manner. Therefore, knowing all of those unpleasant facts about who he is, what he's done, and what lies in his future, that man doesn't have a thing to lose by committing the most vile acts on earth. In fact, with a soul so black, he can think up new, even more despicable things to do that won't make one bit of difference when his Judgment Day comes."

"I—I—I don't s-see a reason f-f-f—"

"Ahhh," Abernathy said with a wicked smile, which looked like a thin line cut by the same knife he twisted within the first few layers of flesh covering Justin's chest. "There's that nervous stammer of yours. I must be making you uncomfortable. I just want you to remember who's in charge of this little coalition."

"Y-Y-You are."

"Excellent. And are you clear on my stance regarding the deaths of lawmen?"

"O-On-Only when necessary."

"That's right. They're only to be shot when necessary." Abernathy released his grip on Justin's shirt, allowing his shoulders to hit the ground and the blade to come away from the shallow wound. "Play this right and we'll both be rich in a short amount of time. You muck things up and I'll put an end to you." He straightened up, sheathed the blade in the hidden scabbard at the small of his back, and then smoothed out the front of his shirt. "I know you're angry with me right now, so let's start fresh in the morning."

"I ain't angry, Mr. Abernathy."

"It's perfectly natural. After all, I did lose my temper just now and threatened you in a most uncivilized way. I apologize. Do you accept my apology?"

"Y-Yes."

"Good." The older man went back to his stool, sat down, and picked up a small china cup that he'd been using to drink the tea he'd brewed a while ago. The tea had long gone cold, but he sipped it as if it had been freshly served to him by a waiter in a fancy suit. "And just so you know, I am fully aware of what you're thinking right now. You're thinking of all the ways you could hurt me, be it in my sleep or one of those times when you've got your rifle and you're several yards behind me."

"No! I w-wouldn't—"

"It's fine," Abernathy interrupted. "Perfectly understandable. Just know that if we continue working together, we can part ways much better for having met each other. And if you intend on bringing me harm, try to do a good job of it. You won't get a second chance."

"I don't know where you got them notions about me from," Justin said once his pulse had stopped racing. "I'm just in it for the money."

"Good. Just so long as we understand each other."

13

Two days later, Slocum rode into the town of Hollister on his own. He and Haresh had been riding steadily to make it there less than half an hour after sundown. Right outside town, they'd separated, and Haresh had gone ahead first, to scout out the saloons for any information on Abernathy. Slocum was heading toward a different destination.

Hollister was the kind of town that was about two steps away from being deserted. All that needed to happen was for a few more locals to get enough gumption to find somewhere else to be so more stray dogs and refuse piles could move in. Ghost towns looked like husks that had died a long time ago. Places like Hollister were more like mangy, flea-bitten mutts that didn't have the good sense to roll over and die.

Like most godforsaken towns, Hollister didn't sleep. As Slocum rode down its widest street, he could hear men shouting and women screaming from just about every direction. Houses were dark and shut tight while saloons were alive with light, laughter, and music. There were businesses, hotels, and other conveniences necessary for a town to be any good to anyone, but those places were locked up tight and guarded by folks who would protect them with their lives. Some good people could be found, even in a place like Hollister. Usually, it just took longer to track one down. Slocum knew where to look in order to find at least one person he could rely on for some good information, and he went there without casting a glance at any of the saloons, cathouses, or gambling dens he passed along the way.

Actually, he did cast more than a glance at one bordello called The Starlight House. He looked at the narrow, three-story building on the corner, climbed down from the saddle, and led his horse to the small lot around back. Girls called down to him every step of the way from a few of the windows on the second and third floors. When he approached the back door, one of them waved at him and said, "Come around to the front, handsome."

"I'd prefer to use the back door."

"You're just the man I've been waiting for! I'd prefer if you use my back door, too!"

Slocum couldn't believe he'd walked into that one. It had been a long day.

"It's locked but not for long, cowboy," the woman shouted. "Stay there and I'll be right down."

Even though he was only kept waiting for a few seconds, Slocum lost his patience and tried the door anyway. It was locked, as promised, which didn't stop him from rattling the handle.

Finally, the door was opened by the same woman who'd been shouting at him from above. She had long, dark brown hair and full lips. Her skin was richly tanned and plenty of it could be seen thanks to the silver corset she wore. The upper portion of her garment cradling her breasts was made of black lace. "I told you to come in around the front," she said. "You're lucky I came down to let you in." She took his elbow and pulled him inside. Rubbing her hand along his muscled forearm, she added, "Or maybe I'm the lucky one."

"I'm here to see Olivia."

"Oh, come now, sugar. I can take care of you just fine."

"I'm sure you can," Slocum said. "But I'm here for Olivia."

She let go of his arm and took half a step back as if she'd just found out he was carrying the pox. They stood in a dark kitchen that still smelled like what Slocum guessed was beef stew. The woman put her hands on her hips and scowled at him as she asked, "What's the matter? You not get yer pecker polished good enough last time so now you wanna complain?"

"No!" Slocum chuckled. "I mean . . . that's not why I'm here."

"Then why do you want to see her? Any man who comes in demanding to see one of the bosses is either unhappy or fishing for a discount. Believe me," she added as some of the former sweetness returned to her face, "I was thinking of cutting you a mighty good deal without any fuss."

Slocum wasn't about to pull away as the working girl pressed against him and slipped one hand between his legs. She smelled of lilacs and a hint of sweat that most likely hadn't come from the earlier day's sun. It was a scent that reached down to the same parts of him she was already stroking. She got even closer to him and purred, "I know another girl that might be a lot more fun if that's what you want. Cost you extra, though."

"I think Mr. Slocum knows what he wants," said someone from the other side of the small room.

The brown-haired woman hopped away from him and spun on the balls of her feet to face the new arrival. A slender woman with almond-shaped eyes and rounded cheeks stood in the doorway leading from the kitchen to the rest of the first floor. Her long, coal black hair hung well past her shoulders, and she wore a black slip with red trim as if it were a full ball gown. Rigid posture and confident steps made her seem like the queen of the castle. Inside the walls of The Starlight House, that's exactly who she was.

"Evenin', Miss Olivia," the brown-haired woman said.

"Hello, Janie."

Slocum touched the brim of his hat and grinned. "Olivia."

Olivia's countenance changed considerably as she smirked and said, "Hello, John."

"So you two know each other?" Janie asked.

Slocum set his saddlebags down and turned around to start rummaging through the cabinets for something to eat. "That's right. It's been a while, though. I was hoping she hadn't forgotten about me. How've you been, Olivia?"

Her steps were short and confident as Olivia moved into the kitchen. Dismissing the other woman with a gentle tap on her shoulder, she waited for Janie to leave the room before saying, "I've been good, John. I wish you would have let me know you were coming."

"Why? So you could have baked me a cake? By the looks of this kitchen, you still don't know how to do much more than boil water."

She stepped up to him and placed a hand on top of the one he'd used to open a cabinet. "You want something cooked for you? Go to a restaurant. You want something sweeter than cake? You come to The Starlight House."

"I need information on some outlaws that have been in these parts recently. I also need a place to sleep where I don't have to do it with one eye open . . . so I came to you."

Olivia smiled. "If I was still in that line of work. This isn't the gambling hall where I was working before."

"No. It's a cathouse. Both are just the places that men of all sorts tend to frequent. And since you deal in keeping track of certain kinds of men so you can sell what you know to the highest bidder, I'd say this place is just your style."

Her lips were painted a deep, velvety red. She drifted close enough to Slocum for him to feel her hot breath on his mouth when she parted those lips and whispered, "We did a lot more than trade information the last time we got together."

Olivia slid gently along his side, wrapping one leg around him to brush it against his inner thigh. Her hand cupped his growing erection just enough for him to feel her touch. Unlike the other woman's clumsy groping, Olivia clung to him like fragrant smoke and touched him in a way that would linger in his thoughts for weeks to come.

"We sure did," he sighed.

Her other hand drifted down to tug at his belt. Since that was his gun belt, Slocum's instinctual response was to snap a hand down and pull hers away. Even though he'd been rougher than he would have chosen, she didn't seem to mind one bit. Olivia's eyes were wide and she drew in a quick, excited breath.

"What are you doing?" he asked.

"Making the most of our reunion. Have I touched a nerve?"

"No. You just surprised me is all."

"Good, because I've only started touching you."

She removed his gun belt and placed it on the closest counter so it was in Slocum's sight and, more important, within his reach. She then turned her attention to loosening his jeans enough for her to slide one hand inside them, all the way down to his stiffening cock. "There you are," she whispered.

"I didn't come for this," Slocum said. Quickly he added, "Not that I mind, but there's business to attend to."

Still massaging his erect penis, she asked, "Business before pleasure?"

"Aw, to hell with it." With that, Slocum shifted his feet and turned her around so he was standing directly in front of her and Olivia's back was against a counter. He leaned forward and kissed her hard. She responded immediately by opening her mouth and easing her tongue into his. Her body was just as he remembered—smooth in all the right spots and firm in others. Olivia's hips writhed beneath his hands, allowing him to feel every muscle working as she ground against him. One leg slid up and down the outside of his thigh, and when he reached around to cup her buttocks in both hands, she let out a welcoming sigh.

Although the blood was rushing through his veins in a current that he could hear, Slocum could also hear the voices of some of the girls as well as a few customers in other parts of the house. "Should we take this somewhere else?"

"This ain't a restaurant, John. Nobody comes here for the kitchen, and if someone does catch sight of us, it'll probably just get them worked up enough to go upstairs with one of the other girls."

"Well then," Slocum said as he lifted her up and set her onto the counter, "let's see what we can do to get someone worked up."

Judging by the dampness between her legs, Olivia was plenty worked up already. Slocum hiked up her skirts and felt all the way up her inner thigh to make that pleasant discovery. She started gnawing on his earlobe, moaning contentedly as he rubbed the lips of her pussy up and down.

"God, you know just how to touch me," she whispered.

The few undergarments she'd been wearing had been easy enough to pull aside. Slocum grabbed hold of them and tugged them off. When one silky piece of fabric snagged between her leg and the edge of the counter, he pulled hard enough to tear it. The sound of ripping fabric sent a shudder through Olivia's body and she spread her legs even farther.

Other voices could be heard in some of the nearby rooms, but he didn't pay them any mind. Overhead, the occasional woman's moan could also be heard as one customer or another was given the night they'd paid good money for. Olivia tugged at Slocum's shirt so she could rub her hands along his bare chest. Slocum got her skirts up all the way to her waist and looked down at the sight of tightly muscled thighs that were already glistening from her dripping pussy. Suddenly, he had the urge to put her in his mouth. Her pussy was wet and inviting, and he knew a few well-placed licks would get Olivia purring like a kitten. Before he could make a move, however, she'd reached down to grab his cock with both hands. Her legs wrapped around him to pull him closer as she guided his rigid pole to her slit.

"Don't make me wait, damn you," she snarled. "Fuck me."

Some women tried to talk dirty at moments like these. Many sounded foolish or just ignorant. Olivia's voice was taut and there was a primal quality to it, her words resonating in a way that made Slocum's erection so powerful it bordered on painful. The only way for it to feel better was to do what she asked and he had no intention of resisting her.

Slocum inched forward and slipped his hands beneath Olivia's ass. As she guided him into her, he lifted her up an inch or so while pulling her closer. That way, when he thrust forward, he buried his cock into her as deep as it could possibly go. Her response was a shuddering moan that echoed within the empty kitchen. It wasn't a large room, and the door had been shut. There was a small, rectangular window built into the door that was occasionally darkened by shadows passing on the other side. One of those shadows lingered for a moment as Slocum tightened his grip on Olivia's backside and pounded into her. She grunted and wrapped her arms around his neck. The shadow whispered something to a companion and moved on.

Soon, Slocum and Olivia fell into a rhythm where he pumped in and out of her and she ground her hips against him. After a few minutes, she took hold of his shoulders and leaned back to stare directly into his eyes. Somewhere along the line, Olivia's blouse had been pulled open just enough for him to make out the curve of her breasts and to glimpse her dark little nipples. The expression on her face was intensely focused, and she leaned back as far as she could while thrusting her hips in short, powerful motions.

Slocum looked down at her sweaty body, running one

hand flat against her tit. As he teased her erect nipple between his thumb and forefinger, he let his eyes wander down to the spot where their bodies joined. His cock was slick with her juices and slid in and out of her like a piston. Her pussy tightened on him as she wrapped her arms and legs around him so he couldn't get away.

Olivia was watching the same show he was. Soon she eased a hand between her thighs, and as he pumped into her again and again, Olivia rubbed her clitoris in small, slow circles. Her eyes closed tightly, and her breaths became trembling moans as her climax swiftly approached. When her muscles started to tense, Slocum pounded into her even harder to give her an orgasm that snapped her head to one side and arched her back.

Slocum expected her to cry out or to scream exotic profanity that could be heard throughout the house. Instead, Olivia grunted and strained as if all those things were lodged in the back of her throat and she was unable to push them out. Rather than fall onto her elbows for support once her pleasure subsided, Olivia started nibbling his neck and kissing his ear.

"What are you up to now?" she whispered as Slocum cupped her tight little ass and picked her up off the counter.

His answer came through action, not words.

As he carried her away from the counter, Olivia hung on to him using both her arms and legs. He was still buried inside her as he turned to get a look at the rest of the kitchen. It was a small, confined space filled mostly by two short counters, a few sets of cupboards, and a potbellied stove. The only flat section of wall space he could find was near the door leading into the rest of the house, so Slocum shuffled over there until Olivia's shoulders bumped against the wall and part of the door.

Once he had her braced there, Slocum began thrusting into her hard enough to knock her backside against the door.

He cushioned her partially with his hands, but Olivia wasn't about to complain. On the contrary, she grabbed him tightly with legs that locked around his waist and hands that drove fingernails into the flesh of his back and shoulders.

"Yes!" she snarled. "Yes!"

Slocum drove every inch of his cock into her pussy, which gripped him tighter than her legs. He kneaded the flesh of her backside with both hands, both to hold her in place as well as to feel the tightness of her body as she writhed in pleasure. Each thrust brought Slocum closer to his own apex. His breath became labored and rough. As his grip tightened on her, Olivia's loosened. At least, her legs loosened enough to drop down toward the floor.

"Put me down," she said.

It took Slocum a moment to collect himself enough to for a single word. "Why?"

"Just do it. Quickly!"

Thinking they'd gotten a visitor that was too close for her comfort, Slocum set her down and stepped back. Rather than try to straighten herself up for an uninvited guest, she placed her hands flat upon his chest and pushed him back until he was stopped by one of the cupboards.

"What are you . . ." Before he could form the entire question, Slocum got his answer.

Olivia lowered herself to her knees and took his cock in her hands. It was still slick with her own moisture, which made it slide easily within her grasp as she pumped her hand back and forth. Soon, her lips were wrapped around the tip of his penis and her tongue was flickering against the sensitive skin on its underside. Slocum reached back to grab on to the cupboard, but even that seemed like it might not be enough to steady him.

Her mouth glided up and down the entire length of his rod while her tongue slid along it from several different angles. When she had only his tip in her mouth, she swirled in fast circles before teasing him by running just the end of her tongue along his shaft. She looked up at him and smiled. When she closed her eyes and started sucking even harder, Slocum reached down to place his hands on either side of her head. That way, he could guide her to speed up or slow down. For the most part, he just let her work her magic.

Before long, his climax started to build. It rolled through him like a storm, causing him to tighten his grip on her and let out a slow, rumbling breath. Olivia slowed to a steady, solid pace. She pressed her tongue against his cock so it slid up and down his shaft with every move of her head. At just the right moment, she licked near the base of his shaft until he exploded in her mouth.

Slocum clenched his eyes shut and emptied into her. She swallowed every drop and even licked him a few more times for good measure. When she was through, she eased her head back and lifted one of her hands to him. Slocum accepted it and helped her to her feet.

"Now," she said while dabbing at the corner of her mouth with a napkin. "Let's get down to business."

14

Olivia's office was on the third floor. It was only about half the size of the kitchen, but felt larger because it wasn't nearly as cluttered. The space was filled with a simple rolltop desk, two chairs, and a small wardrobe in a corner. Elegant wall-paper made the room feel like it was in an entirely different county than the bawdy cathouse they'd walked through to get upstairs. After the door was closed, Olivia invited Slocum to sit in one of the chairs and then walked around her desk to settle onto the other. Her movements were slow and slinky as if she was still feeling the effects of their time in the kitchen.

"Care for a cigar?" she asked.

"Do you still buy those fancy ones shipped all the way from China?"

"They're not Chinese, but they are brought in from that part of the globe."

"Wherever they come from, they're worth the trip."

She smiled graciously and extended a cigar box that was half as large as the normal variety. When she opened the lid, exotic fragrances drifted out from tobacco wrapped in papers flavored with oils blended to complement the dried leaves within. "Take only one, please. If you want more, you'll have to earn them." As soon as Slocum helped himself to a cigar, she playfully snapped the box shut as if she had just missed clipping off the tips of his fingers. "Now, what is this business that brings you all the way to the middle of the wilderness?"

"Wilderness? Sounds to me like you might not be happy here. This place seems to be doing pretty well."

"This establishment *is* doing well, and it does look nice. That's only because I made those things happen. Honestly, I'd rather make those same things happen somewhere else . . . like California or New York City." As she spoke the names of those places, Olivia's face took on a dreamy, blissful quality.

"Or San Antonio?"

Hearing the name of that place, on the other hand, brought her right back to the present. "You just had to mention San Antonio. For a man who's told me countless times that we were even for that, you sure like to bring it up a lot."

Slocum grinned around the cigar that was clenched between his teeth. Having already run it beneath his nose a few times, it was time to make the next step. Some cigars were smoked as a pleasant way to cap off a meal or a day. Ones like these were savored to the point that it almost seemed a shame to burn them. Once he struck a match and touched it to the end of his cigar, he changed that opinion. The flavors shifted as the tobacco was singed and the smoke that drifted through the air was unlike anything he'd smelled for quite a while.

"You're a confident woman, Olivia, but every now and then it's good to be brought down a notch."

"Like when you were shooting your mouth off to that pistol salesman in Amarillo and were too drunk to hit any targets in the little shooting gallery he set up to demonstrate his goods?"

Slocum's face darkened despite the fragrant smoke drifting around him. "That shooting gallery was rigged."

"Right. Those little clay pigeons and paper circles were created to withstand the impact of a bullet."

"Like you said, I was drunk."

"Is that why you nearly blew your own head off trying to pull something from the end of that pistol? What was it? A rock?"

"Could have been. That would explain why I missed."

Olivia was now grinning from ear to ear. "Too bad you had to bet everything in your pockets as well as the shirt off your back on hitting those targets. If you knew the gallery was rigged, perhaps you should have thought better of a plan like that."

"I. Was. Drunk."

"That's right. So you probably don't recall approaching the salesman's daughter later that night while you were without a shirt or any money in your pockets." Tapping her chin, Olivia asked, "Was it her or her father who knocked you on your ass?"

Slocum rolled his eyes, trying to enjoy the cigar since he knew it would be pointless to try and get her to let up on him. "It was both. First the daughter knocked me down, and when I got up, that cheating salesman finished me off."

"That's right! Amarillo. What a beautiful town. Such delightful memories."

"Your point's made, Olivia."

"Good thing I was there to get you out of that jail cell," she continued. "If you weren't such a good lover, I might not have bothered looking around to find out why you didn't show up to meet me afterward." Folding her hands on top of her desk and grinning at him in a way that was annoying but still very pretty, she said, "You're right. It is good to bring someone down a notch."

"Can we get back to business now?"

"I suppose."

"You still keep abreast on who wanders through your territory?" Slocum asked.

She raised her eyebrows and steepled her fingers. "*My* territory? You're giving me a lot of credit."

"I don't mean Montana. I mean your . . . what did you call it back in Texas? That's right. Your sphere of influence. Do you still keep abreast of who crosses into your sphere of influence?"

"I was a bad girl when you found me, John."

"And judging by what we cooked up in that kitchen downstairs, you're still a bad girl."

"I help manage the girls here and balance the books," she said. "If a fellow who fancies himself a lawman comes around trying to clean up this town, I'm the first one to greet him."

"People have come to clean up this town?" Slocum asked.

"They've tried. If I can't convince them otherwise . . . well . . . bad things happen to them. I don't have anything to do with that, of course," she quickly added. "This town is full of violent men."

"Which brings me back to my first question. Back in Texas, you made certain to get a good feel for the comings and goings of violent men." Slocum took a puff of his cigar and sent some of the exotic smoke toward the ceiling.

"Not just violent men," she corrected. "Also rich ones."

"That's right. You sold information to bounty hunters, saloon owners, men who ran big card games, anyone who might pay for that sort of knowledge. Quite a good way to make a lot of money. Plenty of people looking for those types of men."

"Also a good way to get run out of Texas."

"That's right," Slocum said in a tone that wasn't at all meant to rub her nose in the misfortunes of her past. "Even so, you had quite an operation going. I'd be surprised to find out you chucked it all so you could work in this wild territory as nothing more than a madam."

Letting out a tired sigh, Olivia reached for the cigar box and helped herself to one. She took a match from a small metal container, lit it, and then indulged in a long puff. Even though she wasn't trying to entice him, Slocum couldn't help admiring the way her lips wrapped around that cigar.

"I had a good idea, and yes, I had a good operation going," she told him. "But that was because I had a lot of friends in Texas, including a lot of saloon keepers as well as a few federal marshals who owed me a whole lot of favors. I spread some money around, paid for information, and got paid more for it by men who knew they could trust me to be discreet and not let anyone know they'd been discovered or try to sell out the ones who'd bought my information in the first place. It was a tangled web that took a lot of time to weave. I don't have that kind of thing going here."

"But you're still Olivia Caster."

"What's that supposed to mean?"

Slocum puffed his cigar and blew the smoke to one side. "It means you're a talented and capable woman who made some good money providing a very popular service."

She exhaled as well, her smoke blending with what Slocum had contributed a few seconds ago. "You could say that about the job I've got now."

"You're also a smart woman, Olivia. Too smart to ditch a good thing so you can watch over a cathouse. You being you, I'm thinking you've already made some influential friends or started gathering valuable information. After all, this is just the sort of place where men might say things they wouldn't say anywhere else or part with information while trying to impress a pretty woman."

"Do men seriously try to impress whores?" she asked. "After all, what's the point?"

"There is no point, but yes. Men still do try to impress a woman even if she is bought and paid for. It's a reflex."

Olivia grinned in a way that showed she was a little surprised that he had such insight into the failings of his own gender. "All right. So what if I have been making a few friends since I've been in this territory?"

"Then you might be able to help me. I'm looking for a man named Ferril Abernathy."

"Far Eye Abernathy?"

"That's the one."

She chuckled and kicked her feet up onto the corner of her desk. "You should have said so at the start. We could have avoided all of this cat-and-mouse nonsense."

"You guard your sources carefully, Olivia. After all we've done for each other . . . all we've done *to* each other . . . you still haven't told me any specific places where you get your information. I guessed you might even try to play off this move to Montana as some sort of fresh start."

"It is." With a shrug, she added, "Of a sort."

"Right. You got to disappear from whoever was looking for you after finding out you'd pointed someone in their direction and can start fresh with a bunch of mountain men and trappers who will keep their eyes and ears open for you because you're the pretty new lady in town. Am I close?"

"Maybe, but you still didn't have to go through so much trouble to hear anything about Far Eye Abernathy. He's a legend."

"Then why haven't I heard of him?"

"I'll bet you have and don't even know it." Before Slocum could protest, Olivia held up a hand and said, "He started off doing displays for a few circuses that traveled from California all the way out to the Dakota Territories. Made a name for himself doing trick shots and then one day someone comes in to steal the money from the till."

Slocum snapped his fingers. "I heard something along those lines once! The robber was Dave Corcoran, wasn't it? He'd been tearing through a bunch of towns leaving bodies piled all over the place and so he told that trick shot artist to go to hell. The artist stands his ground, Corcoran turns his gun on him, and the artist burns him down. That was Abernathy?"

With a single nod, Olivia said, "About ten years ago. What about that gang from New Mexico that was holed up in the town without a sheriff? Maybe you heard that one, too. Once the gang was there, nobody could get anyone to pick up a badge and defend the place and nobody was allowed to leave to get help."

"And there was one man who walked into town," Slocum said. "Called them all out and shot them down like he was knocking cans off the top rail of a fence. That's another legend. You can't walk into any saloon in New Mex without hearing someone tell that old tale."

"Well, it's true and Abernathy was the man who strode into town."

"There's no way you could know that," Slocum scoffed.

"When you're in my line of work, listening to stories is part of the job. You learn how to separate the truth from everything else and get a knack for putting a picture together when enough pieces fall into place. I've been hearing things like this for years. Anyone running a saloon in Texas did. After a while, enough pieces came together for me to believe some of the things about Abernathy. Also," she added while tapping the ash from her cigar, "it didn't hurt that he strutted around like a cock of the walk wherever he went and never really stopped performing his craft."

"You mean gunning people down?"

"I saw him silence a man with a big mouth who thought he was calling Far Eye's bluff. It was some of the best shooting I've ever seen."

"He's a killer."

Olivia shook her head. "Not that day. The man and one of his friends called Far Eye out in front of half the town, swearing up a storm until all that was left to do was fight. Far Eye waited for *them* to draw first and then emptied his pistol into them. One bullet into each of their feet and one for each of their gun hands. Each shot, dead center. Even the sheriff had to applaud when he arrived to clean up the mess."

Slocum let the smoke roll around in his mouth as he put together some pieces of his own. The more he thought about those stories, the more familiar they seemed. "You know . . . I heard tell of a man who collected a bounty by waiting outside of a bank and picking off the robbers one by one. There were four robbers and the man who picked them off did his waiting a hundred and fifty yards away from the bank. One or two from that distance isn't too bad, but four in a row when they must have scattered in separate directions is quite the feat."

"Where did that happen?" she asked.

"New Mexico."

"See? You just added one more story to the legend of Far Eye Abernathy."

"I forgot all about that one until you got me thinking. May not even be Abernathy."

Olivia grinned and placed her cigar between her lips. "Part of my job is getting the wheels turning. Next time someone asks about that bank display, I'll have something to tell them."

"Which could get more wheels turning?" Slocum asked.

She merely shrugged and grinned.

"So you do know something about Abernathy?" he asked.

"Just a whole lot of stories."

"Not those. I mean something more current. Like where I might be able to find him."

After thinking for a second, Olivia told him, "I heard he broke someone out of a jail not too far from here. One of those little camps in the mountains."

"More current than that."

When she heard that sentence, Olivia leaned forward ever so slightly and her eyes genuinely seemed to sparkle with a light of their own. "So you already know about the jail break?"

"A lot of people must know about it by now."

"You were there."

Since she told him that without even coming close to it being a question, Slocum's first reaction was to say, "Yes, and you're right. It was some of the finest shooting I've ever seen."

"So Far Eye still has the touch. That's good to know."

"Christ Almighty. How much else did you pull out of me from what I've said in this room?"

"Nothing that will come back to bite you," she said with a wink. "And don't feel too badly if you said something you didn't mean to say. I've cracked much tougher men than you with a whole lot less. As for where to find Far Eye now, if that really was him who broke that man out of jail, it shouldn't be too difficult to find someone who's heard or seen something since then."

"So you weren't even sure that was him behind the jail break?"

"Not until you confirmed it. Like I said. It's all part of my job."

Raising his cigar as if it were a wineglass, Slocum said, "Then here's to a job well done."

"Are you in town all by yourself?"

"What? You didn't think to ask that earlier?"

Olivia's cheeks flushed with some color that fell just short of being a true blush. "I guess I pounced on you pretty quickly downstairs, didn't I? Well, it's been a long time, and seeing you was a surprise. Someone in my line of work doesn't get surprised very often."

"I'll try to do it again. I'm not in town alone. I'm riding with a man named Haresh. Ever heard of him?"

"Haresh? What is that?"

"I think it's East Indian."

"No," she snapped. "First or last name?"

Slocum furrowed his brow and admitted, "I'm not quite sure. It's always just been . . . Haresh."

"What's he look like?"

He gave her a detailed description of the big man, and

Olivia listened as if she was absorbing every syllable of every word. He followed up by telling her everything else he knew about Haresh. It didn't take long.

"What do you want from me where this man is concerned?" she asked.

"I want to know if he's more than he says he is or if he's got any dirt under his fingernails."

"Everyone's got dirt under their nails, John."

"You know what I mean," he said. "He's riding with me to try and find Abernathy."

"And where is he now?"

"We split up outside of town," Slocum told her. "He works at a saloon, so I told him to scout out the saloons here in town for word about Abernathy. Judging by the way he looked at me when we parted ways, he might think I plan on leaving him here."

Olivia made an exaggerated pouting expression and said, "It's been my experience that you do tend to run off."

Rather than take that bait, Slocum merely scowled at her.

"All right. I don't blame you for leaving me in Texas. So what has Abernathy done to get you so riled up?"

"Killed a few people in front of me for no good reason. He also may be riding with some other killers."

That perked Olivia up. "Really? And who might they be?"

"Never mind about them. Right now, let's get back to Haresh."

"Partnering up with you on something like this could be dangerous. Does he have good reason to go through all that trouble? I find that question gets some of the most interesting answers."

Slocum nodded. "I'll have to keep that in mind. It would sure do me a lot of good if I had your knack where digging up information is concerned."

Standing up and setting her cigar on the edge of a ceramic ashtray, she said, "You need to stay in one place long enough to become a harmless fixture, and I don't see you ever doing that. Also," she added while sliding her hands along her hips, "it doesn't hurt if you can fill out a dress as well as this."

"Afraid I fall short on both counts," Slocum said. "Think you can help me with my business proposition?"

"It's not a business proposition until there's some kind of profit involved. What's in it for me?"

"Remember how you tried to wheedle all those names and dates from me when we were in Texas?" he asked.

"I was just asking about the gunmen that seem to be drawn to you like flies to manure. Even though you've buried more men than anyone can count, you didn't want to talk about a single one. Told me you didn't like the notion of helping bounty hunters."

Slocum stood up as well. "I don't keep accurate details on everything I've done, but I can set aside some time where we can talk about anything you like, and in that time, I'll answer anything you want about anyone you want."

"Anyone?"

"I won't put anyone in danger who doesn't belong there," he clarified.

"So far, I've only got a few bounty hunters that I deal with. The rest are lawmen who either work in the territory or are passing through trying to drag someone out of the mountains. Anyone those men are after isn't worth protecting."

"What about vigilantes?" Slocum asked. "You must get approached by plenty of them."

"Not at first, but once I told one of them where to find a man who kidnapped a little girl last fall, they've been coming out of the woodwork. They can be tightly wound, but usually their hearts are in the right place." Seeing the suspicious rise of Slocum's eyebrow, she added, "If they're after someone who doesn't already have a price on their head or isn't someone I know is a piece of scum, all I have to do is tell them I haven't heard anything and they back away."

"What happens if they don't back away?"

She walked around her desk and rubbed his cheek. "Worried about me, John? That's sweet. Before I started bartering information, I made sure to surround myself with friends that can protect me."

"Like you had me protect you in Texas?"

"That's right," she said. "And if you recall, I handled a situation or two on my own just fine as well."

"You did. So do we have a deal?"

Her expression hardened into that of a shrewd businesswoman. "Give me two hours of your time?"

"Half an hour."

"One hour?"

"Done," Slocum said.

She shook his hand. "I'll see what I can dig up about your friend, the mysterious Mr. Haresh."

15

Ferril Abernathy rode into town alone. This was nothing new to him, but the manner in which he made his appearance felt very strange indeed. Night was falling and rather than dress in his usual expensive, well-tailored suits, black hat, and polished boots, he'd donned a set of clothes that he referred to as "grubby and mediocre." To just about anyone else who rode into Hollister from the surrounding wilderness, the semirumpled white shirt, battered brown jacket, and simple trousers would still seem a little fancy. The brim on his hat was wide enough to keep his face mostly covered as he rode through town and looked for a good place to put up his horse for a day or two. Since he quickly realized "good" might be a stretch, he lowered his standards and left his horse at a place that looked somewhat clean.

From there, he strolled about town, getting a feel for the streets and watching for lawmen. There weren't many officials, but nearby there seemed to be men with cautious eyes and hands that never strayed far from their gun belts.

Vigilantes.

If he was a betting man, Ferril would have laid a healthy

sum on that guess. While in the Montana Territory, it behooved a man like Abernathy to be able to spot a vigilante from as far away as possible. It did him even more good to keep that much distance between him and the self-righteous murderers who all but ruled the area with the proverbial iron fist.

But it wasn't them he was worried about. Lawmen and self-important animals with guns were a constant thorn in his side. He was in Hollister to meet with a few very important people, and once he'd gotten what he was after, it was on to California. After that . . . even he didn't know. For someone who'd planned his life out almost to the second and then made it his obsession to see those plans through, that much uncertainty was a refreshing change.

He smiled at the prospects looming in front of him. Naturally, when a woman passing him by saw the cheery expression on his face, she answered with a smile of her own. Ever the gentleman, Ferril removed his hat and turned on his heel so he could change direction and fall into step beside her.

"Good evening to you, ma'am."

"Good evening," she replied while trying to hide her smile.

"I was wondering if you could direct me to the Cat's Eye."

Her smile fell away like dried mud that had been shaken from someone's boot after a good, hard tap. "Down the street and right at the corner. You'll find it next to the rest of the opium dens run by that horrible Chinese man."

"Is that a safe place at this time of night?"

The woman gazed up at the sky. Although there were still strips of deep purple amid the spreading blackness overhead, she winced as if she were looking up at the cold, inky sprawl of infinity. "Probably not. Lord only knows what sort of men are staggering about, out of their minds."

Abernathy nodded sympathetically, but in truth he was holding back a smile. When he saw someone display a nagging fear or grating dislike toward something, he found it amusing to goad them a bit. It was like poking at a sensitive patch of skin just to watch the other person jump. To those who were above such fears and hatreds, it was an amusing display.

"I imagine it's terrible," he said. "Such a shame that their kind has to invade such a nice place like this."

"Yes! It is. It truly is." Her face brightened and she looked at Abernathy as if she'd known him for months. "Are you new in town?"

Abernathy couldn't help thinking that he could have his way with this woman. She was already on the hook and wanted badly to be reeled in. After years of spotting potential audience members for his circus acts and drawing suckers to the conmen who traveled with those shows, he'd become adept at picking up on such things. If he had more time, he might even enjoy bringing this catch to a dark room and having a tasty snack. Instead, he nodded and said, "I am, indeed. Unfortunately, I have matters to attend to in that unsavory district you spoke of. If you'd like to accompany me . . ."

Asking that woman to walk with him to the place that she so recently regarded with disgust was the quickest way to turn her stomach. She turned away with a snippy refusal of his offer. Abernathy watched her walk away, imagining what could have been. She wasn't much to look at, but had a few inviting curves here and there. Then again, that could have also been a trick of her poorly fitted dress. He turned toward the direction she'd indicated and continued walking.

Entering another district in a town the size of Hollister was a simple matter of walking for a few minutes in one direction. People bustled here and there, winding between dogs, cats, and carts pulled by tired horses. Now that the sunlight was gone, saloons were gathering momentum and strangers would be anxious to find rooms for the night. Part of that bustle was an illusion, however, created by tight, meandering streets clogged by vendor stalls and buildings that had been built too close together. Ferril took it all in and quickly detected the scent of exotic smokes coming from shacks and large tents marked by signs bearing tigers, dragons, and lotus blossoms.

Between what the fidgety woman had told him and his understanding of Oriental markings, Abernathy didn't have much trouble in finding the Cat's Eye. It was a squat building that was twice as long as it was wide. The door was guarded by a large man wearing a gun belt, which wasn't anything unusual. More than likely, that man was mainly there to keep an eye on all the other armed men standing outside of the other nearby businesses. Abernathy approached the door, tipped his hat, and started walking in. He was stopped by an arm that stretched out to block his path like a bar of iron.

"No guns inside," the man said.

Abernathy playfully replied, "You're wearing a gun."

"I'm not inside."

"Fair enough. How about, after I meet with the owner of this place, I bring you out something warm to drink?"

The guard wasn't in the mood to banter. That much was made clear by the deadly glare he shot at Abernathy.

"I hear there are unsavory characters inside and I need to protect myself," Abernathy said. "Surely we could arrange—"

"I said no guns. Either leave them with me or get the hell out of my sight."

Unfortunately, the guard had not only proven to be unmovable but was also observant enough to pick up on the fact that Abernathy wore two pistols beneath the coat that covered everything but a glimpse of the gun belt's buckle. "All right," he said while opening his coat and unbuckling the holster. "Rules are rules."

As he went through the motions of handing over the .44s, another armed man appeared from one of the shadows to make sure he didn't try anything foolish. Having noticed the man lurking there when he'd arrived, Abernathy looked at him now as if he was surprised by the arrival. "My goodness! Is there more going on in there than what I smell?"

"People can get wild if they ain't used to smoking that stuff," the first guard said. "If that happens, you'll be glad we're here and even gladder that we take everyone's guns from them."

As one last attempt at humor, Abernathy asked, "What if I intend to be one of those wild men?"

The guard looked him up and down to take his stock. The dry chuckle that scraped in the back of his throat made it clear he wasn't impressed. "If you want to stay healthy, I'd advise you sit on yer pillow, smoke yer stuff, and go to sleep like everyone else."

"Sound advice. Much obliged."

The guard handed over the .44s to the one who'd stepped out of the shadows and used his other hand to wave Ferril in through the front door. Abernathy went where he was told and was greeted by a friendly woman dressed in a faded red silk slip. To the locals, Abernathy thought, she must appear quite striking.

"Welcome to Cat's Eye," she said in a thick Chinese accent. "Have you been here before?"

"I haven't."

"Then you would like me to show you to a room? I can recommend something you will like very much."

"I don't think so."

"Then you already know what you like?"

"Yes," Abernathy said. "I would like a word with the manager."

Her face took on a pacifying quality that grated against his nerves worse than a rake being dragged across dry slate. "If there is a problem, I'm sure I can handle it," she assured him. "If you would like something other than what is on the menu," she said while motioning toward a locked cabinet that was surely filled with the narcotics that were burning in the rooms behind her, "then I can help you as well." She eased up to him and placed a delicate hand upon his chest just above his heart. It was an attempt to both endear herself to him and titillate him at the same time. "Surely I can help you in ways that the manager cannot." Abernathy had worked in plenty of gambling halls with saloon girls, and that was one of their most common methods short of simply allowing their blouses to fall open at the right time.

"I'm sure you could." He reached up as if to take her hand like any would-be suitor. Although it appeared to be a simple enough gesture, the pressure he applied on the nerves in her wrist using only a few bony fingers sent a jolt of pain through her entire body. "I've already asked you politely. Now take me to Mr. Baynes before I become . . . impolite."

She tried twisting out of his grasp, but failed. When she began to look toward another part of the room where there were surely guards watching, Abernathy applied just enough pressure to stop her. "You'd better look as if you're still trying to wrangle me into an overpriced bowl of opium," he warned. "Otherwise you may lose this pretty little hand."

Her smile may have been strained, but it appeared genuine enough to anyone watching from more than a few paces away. For once, her ability to feign pleasure wasn't an asset. "Let me go," she said quietly, "and I will take you." When Abernathy released her, she rubbed her wrist and smiled graciously. They walked side by side down a narrow hall that was lined on both sides with several skinny doors. The rooms behind those doors were probably no bigger than closets. For the men who came to have their lives and burdens melted away by the opium they inhaled, all they needed was enough room to collapse onto a pile of blankets and cheap pillows.

"If you are planning to rob us, you are making a mistake," she told him under her breath. "You'll never make it out of here alive."

"I'm no robber."

"Mr. Baynes will kill you. He has killed many men."

"I've killed more," Abernathy replied quickly. When she looked over to him, he showed her enough confidence in his eyes to tell her he meant what he said.

"There is not much money here," she said weakly.

"Just shut up and show me where the office is," he snapped. "If you'd been more helpful at the start, none of this would have been necessary."

Sufficiently discouraged from saying any more, the woman led him to an office at the end of the hall. They were just far enough from the rest of the rooms for the pungent, semisweet smoke to be more of an afterthought in the back of his nose than the overpowering haze from before. She knocked twice on the door and then knocked again. Abernathy rolled his eyes at the clumsy signal and shoved her into the door hard enough to force it open. The man behind the shoddy desk was still in the process of removing a gun from a drawer when he and the woman stepped inside.

The expression on the man's face was a mix of anger and surprise. A second later, it lost its edge. "That you, Ferril?"

"It sure is. How are you, Lester?"

"You . . . know him?" the woman asked.

Abernathy stepped over to a liquor cabinet and poured himself a drink. The office wasn't exactly spacious, but felt comfortable compared to the cramped hallway and equally cramped streets of Hollister. "She's very astute," he said while nodding toward the Chinese woman. "You should hire more just like her."

"I've got plenty more like her on my payroll," Baynes said. "Perhaps I could introduce you."

"I must go," the woman said distastefully. "Someone has to be up front to greet customer."

"Right, go on ahead," Baynes said. "Give us a little while to talk and then send in one of the other girls. Is Chen working tonight?"

"Yes."

"Good. Send her." To Abernathy, he said, "You'll like Chen. Just the sort of China doll someone expects in a place like this."

Abernathy was about to refuse the offer, but took a moment to consider it. "That . . . could be nice. It's been a while since I've sampled some of the finer things from the Orient."

"I will send her," the woman said. "Later." She couldn't get out of the room fast enough and slammed the door behind her.

"She's a peach," Baynes said.

Now that his first sip of gin was down, Abernathy replied, "Seemed dense and cheap to me."

"Trust me. She ain't cheap. What brings you to Hollister?"

Turning his back to a wall so he could see Baynes and the door without turning his head, Abernathy said, "You know why I'm here."

"You still chasing after that damn California job? I told you before, it's an old wives' tale. There ain't no depot where all them little bits of gold are brought in from so many different places."

"It's got to go somewhere once it's sold."

"Sure, but an entire storeroom filled with everything from dust to nuggets as big as your fist? The only places carrying that much gold are forts and armored train cars. You ain't never had the inclination to rob any of those. You've always been more of a finesse man."

"I still am," Abernathy said with an appropriately showy wave of his hand. "That's why I'm not intending to do something as brutish as rob a train or shoot my way into a bank vault. The storeroom in question is guarded by more than just guns. It takes someone with comparable intelligence to get inside. Since you've known me for many years, you should know I have such an intellect."

"You always were a smart one. But still, I didn't think you'd buy into the myth of some room full of gold sitting in California. That ain't more than . . ."

"A legend?" Abernathy said. "Well, so am I, my friend. When people speak about the things I've done in my years while performing and in the years since, many of them insist it's nothing but tall tales and legend. I am not a gullible man. I assure you I am going off of much more than word of mouth. It has taken me years to track down enough clues to tell me where this storeroom is and even more effort to figure out what's needed to crack it open. It exists and I almost have what I need to get the job done."

"Almost," Baynes said with a grin. "That's why you're here, right?"

"Precisely. Do you still have those chemicals you used to use to put people to sleep?"

"People and elephants. Remember when the circus rolled into—"

"Can we continue our reminiscing later?" Abernathy asked. "It's been a long day."

"Sure." Baynes walked over to join him at the liquor cabinet. He poured himself a drink, sipped it, and swirled the remainder in his glass. "You really found that storeroom?"

Abernathy nodded. "It's used as a collection point for businesses and small buyers who work with large mines all the way down to tin panners who get cheated by the blowhards in their local dry goods store. The gold is collected and sold off in bulk to larger buyers, including government officials and representatives from foreign lands. I would imagine smaller buyers like jewelers and such are accommodated as well, but those details aren't important. Gold has to go somewhere after it's mined and this is one of those places. The only place it goes from there that I care about is my own pockets. What I need from you are chemicals to put a sizable number of people to sleep for a specific amount of time."

"Couldn't you find that somewhere else? I mean, that may

take a certain amount of skill to mix, but there are plenty of chemists out there."

"Not any that I could rely upon to keep my needs a secret. Especially when I also need a mixture that will mimic death and another that's genuinely fatal. The final mixture I require is a simple concoction that can produce euphoric and hallucinatory effects. That one," Abernathy said while sweeping an arm toward the door that led to the rest of the building, "I'm certain you can hand over to me right now."

Baynes swirled his gin in its glass. "That's a tall order, Ferril. Must be one hell of a convoluted scheme you've worked up."

"I've had plenty of time to think it over."

"Sometimes simpler is better, you know."

Abernathy grinned. "I've always been drawn to the dramatic. Part of my showman's ways."

"You're putting your life on the line with this job. The more moving parts you set in motion, the more there is to go wrong."

"You're not the first to tell me that. I've been putting my life on the line quite a bit since the circus was closed down. So far, it's worked out pretty well."

After taking another sip of gin to steel himself, Baynes asked, "And what happens when it doesn't work out? All it takes is one slip and your show's over for good."

"No need to speak to me like I'm a child, Lester. I was the one to teach you how to fire a pistol when you first started traveling with the circus, remember?"

"Then maybe it's my turn to look out for you. I've heard about some of the things you been up to in the last few years. I know you well enough to believe some of them stories are true. You're a demon with them pistols. If you want gold, why not just crack open something smaller like a bank or some rich man's safe?"

"Look at me. I may be dashing and suave as ever, but I'm getting old. I've spent too much time performing my tricks against real opponents and not enough in creating a nest egg to see me through my golden years. A job like this is just what I need for a farewell performance."

"With the emphasis on performance." Baynes leaned against the liquor cabinet, his weight making the piece of furniture groan as if it was going to collapse at any second. "You were a showman before you signed up for the circus, you lapped up every second of glory when you were traveling with us, and I imagine you're still a showman now. All that's missing is the big top over your head."

"All the world's a stage."

"You can quote all the fancy scripture you want," Baynes grunted. "It still seems clear to me that whatever you've concocted where this gold is concerned ain't nothing more than another performance. You need money? You can steal all you want using them guns. Hell, you could still put on a show yourself and charge good money for tickets. That should be enough to put some food on yer table."

"It's about more than feeding myself," Abernathy told him.

"Whatever it's about, you need to watch your step. Are you working alone?"

"Not all the time."

"Whoever your partners are, they could be in danger, too." Dropping his voice to a harsh whisper, he added, "I could be in danger if it gets back to anyone about why you came to see me. What have you got planned for so many chemicals anyway?"

Abernathy smiled like a preacher reflecting on the great beyond. "That needn't concern you, my friend. Everything is well in hand."

"Be that as it may," Baynes replied like an unconvinced member of the congregation, "whoever you approached to get . . . whatever the hell else you need to pull this off . . . they'll be in danger, too. And what happens after you do this job? That is, assuming you actually pull it off. You think your partners will just take their share, thank you, and be on their way? Men that do this sort of thing are out for all the money they can get, and the easiest way to get more is to shoot one of their partners in the back when the hard part's over. I've heard plenty of them sorts of stories."

"You've been listening to too much gossip," Abernathy said. The grin on his face let Baynes know the irony of that statement hadn't gone unnoticed. "Trust me. I can handle myself and I can surely handle any partners I may have brought along. In fact, one of my partners has already been handled. For what's left of my road to California, I don't need to replace him."

"And what about the law?" Baynes asked in a low voice that was again more of a whisper, as if he was afraid of eavesdroppers lurking in every corner. "I don't even mean the kind that wear a badge. I'm talking about vigilantes."

"Since when are they considered the law?" Abernathy scoffed.

"They are in these parts. They're to be feared a hell of a lot more than any marshal or sheriff. Vigilantes have more pull in this territory than in any other. Some of them are batshit crazy and they don't have to follow any rules. I'd hate to see you buried by the likes of them."

Although Abernathy lifted his glass to his lips, he didn't drink. Instead, he sniffed the cheap liquor and closed his eyes before finally pouring some of it into his mouth. He let it set there for a spell before swallowing it. "I've lived a long time and have seen plenty of ups and downs. For the last several years . . . more downs than ups. Either way, this job will be my last. When it's over, no matter how it turns out, people will remember Ferril Abernathy as a true legend. So . . . will you help me or not?"

"I suppose," Baynes sighed. "I'll need a few days to mix up them chemicals. Also, even if I cut you a deal for old times' sake, it'll cost you plenty."

"Get to work."

16

The next morning, Hollister felt more alive than anyplace Slocum had been for the last few months. Slocum made his way out of The Starlight House and was immediately swept up in the tide of folks navigating the winding streets. If there was any rhyme or reason in how those streets been laid out, Slocum had yet to figure it out. Contrary to how a settlement should be planned, the pathways had been created after the buildings, tents, and vendor carts had all staked their claim on the available land. As he joined the flow of humanity streaming through town, Slocum was reminded of ants swarming across a dirty floor. At first, they all seemed to be moving at random. Upon closer inspection, he could make out several different lines of the little critters moving, curving, and intersecting into one big picture. It was into that sort of organized chaos that Slocum had now been tossed.

Since he didn't have a particular destination in mind, Slocum was able to let himself be carried along like a leaf that had fallen on top of a rushing stream. He was jostled, bumped, prodded, pushed, and shoved nearly every step of the way. By the time he spotted a small restaurant at a nearby corner, he was ready to start throwing elbows just to get a moment or two where he wasn't treated like damn cattle in a chute.

He didn't see the name of the restaurant before stumbling in through the front door that was held open like a trap set by the owner intended to scoop up some customers. The whiff of frying bacon Slocum caught as he'd gotten close to the place was the most pleasant and effective bait he could imagine.

"Good morning!" said a cheerful woman in her early forties. Bright, blond hair framed her face in bouncy curls. She was dressed simply, but possessed a natural beauty that made her shine no matter what was wrapped around her. "Hope you're hungry."

"I sure am. I'll take some of that bacon I smell."

"Anything else to go with that? Maybe some biscuits, eggs, or oatmeal?"

"Keep the oatmeal," Slocum said. "Send out some of the rest, though. Have any coffee?"

"No, but I can brew some up right quick."

"Even better!" he said with a smile that almost matched the one worn by the blond woman. Almost, but not quite.

The restaurant was a small place with about half of its ten tables occupied. It was a long, narrow building with the kitchen all the way in the back, leaving the dining area on display thanks to a wide window spanning the entire front wall. No matter where he sat, Slocum felt exposed. He settled at a table where his back was to a wall, but just about anyone walking on the street could spot him inside. Even if he moved to a table farther inside the place, it wouldn't have helped. The restaurant was so small that it might as well have been a stage thanks to that one huge window.

Slocum considered trying his luck at another place. That idea left him when he pulled in another breath laden with the thick scent of bacon. When he thought about the coffee being brewed for him, Slocum decided to sit tight and take his chances. That turned out to be a good move when Haresh walked past the front window. The big man wasn't being jostled as much as Slocum had, but it still took some work for him to separate from the crowd and step into the restaurant. He dusted himself off while making his way to Slocum's table, looking very much like he'd been dragged to the establishment behind a runaway stagecoach.

"There you are," Haresh said.

Slocum offered him a chair by kicking it a few inches away from his table. "Here I am. Awfully lucky for you to catch sight of me through that window from the mess outside."

"Not too lucky. I was shouting your name ever since you left that hotel."

"What?"

"Have you gone deaf?" Haresh snapped. "Maybe that explains why you didn't hear me outside."

"I didn't hear you outside because it's crazy out there for some reason."

"There's a logging camp a mile from here," Haresh said. "Three of them, actually. Is that coffee?"

Before Slocum could get too confused about the sudden change of subject, he saw the blond woman approach the table carrying a tall kettle and a cup. "It *is* coffee," she said. "Would you like some?"

"Yes," Haresh replied with a wide grin. "Very much."

"I'll be right back with your cup."

The instant she turned away from the table, Slocum asked, "What's this about a logging camp? Did someone there tell you where I was staying?"

"No. The logging camp is giving its men a few days off while they're repairing some broken equipment. One of the other camps just had a payday and the third is preparing to push into some new forests."

"What's that got to do with anything?" Slocum asked.

"That is why the town is so crowded this morning," Haresh stated simply.

Slocum felt stunned as the picture that hadn't made a lick of sense all this time suddenly became clear. "How'd you find out about that?"

"You asked me to visit the saloons. Saloon keepers know all about those sorts of things. Any business owner here would know about the logging camps."

"Oh, that's such a mess, isn't it?" the waitress said as she returned with Haresh's cup. "Between all the supplies being bought and folks coming here looking for work at one of them camps, it's like a jungle out there. I'm not looking forward to tonight. Once all those rowdy loggers come in to spend their pay, this place will be torn up by the roots! Would you care for anything to eat?"

Haresh ordered a breakfast that was more than twice the size of Slocum's. Sensing the anxiousness radiating from Slocum like heat from a fire, the waitress patted his shoulder and said, "I can tell you're starving, so yours will be out as soon as I can get it."

"Appreciate it," Slocum said. After she left, he was feeling better. Even so, there was a definite edge to his voice when he asked, "So how did you know where I was staying?"

Haresh smirked. "One of the saloons I went to for information about finding anyone who might know about Abernathy directed me to the bordellos. They also mentioned the Chinese district. It seems many of the bounty hunters that come through here learn much from men after their guard is dropped from smoking too much opium. I did find out some interesting things, one of which was from a man who was visiting a whorehouse next door to the gambling parlor I was in. Apparently, someone at that whorehouse was unable to wait to get upstairs before having his way with his woman."

"Aw, hell."

"This man had his way with a woman in the kitchen, of all places."

"Enough about that," Slocum growled.

"So modest," Haresh chuckled, "I find that surprising. Anyway, since you decided to roam this place on your own last night, I had time to look into that bordello in case one of the girls there might have seen Far Eye Abernathy. They always have such colorful tales to tell."

"Yeah," Slocum sighed. "I bet."

"One of them mentioned hearing the name *Slocum*. Perhaps it was called out in a moment of passion from that delightful kitchen?"

Hoping to cut the topic short, Slocum asked, "And she also told you where I was staying?"

"I couldn't find you and was getting tired, so I came back this morning. I was on my way to pay you a visit when you stepped out and came here. As I told you already, I shouted your name every step of the way."

Slocum rubbed his temple to try and soothe the ache that was forming there. Sometimes he preferred a gunfight to the sneaking around required when tracking someone in this fashion. Not only did he have to be concerned with being spotted by Abernathy and anyone connected to him, but he also had to worry about the wrong person overhearing him when he was catching up with an old friend like Olivia. Certainly catching up with her wasn't exactly quiet, but he hadn't counted on it getting back to Haresh.

Finally, Slocum drank some of his coffee and said, "Well, I guess you did your job a lot better than I thought you would."

"I will take that as a compliment."

"Fine. Did you learn anything about someone other than me while you were out and about last night?"

"I did. Word has spread about the jail break from Tarnish Mills, as well as the fighting that occurred at Jocelyn's place in Spencer Flats."

"That's bound to happen, right?"

"Not as quickly as this," Haresh said definitively. "And not in as much detail as I heard in several saloons around here. It took us a few days to ride in from Spencer Flats and we were going as fast as we could."

"We didn't see much of anyone along that trail," Slocum added. "That's not to say that there couldn't have been anyone else taking a different trail, but it does seem suspicious."

"More than suspicious. I think Abernathy is here in town as we speak and that he was riding fast enough to beat us here. All but one of the saloons I went to last night knew about the jail break and what happened at Jocelyn's. They even knew a man had been gunned down after the smoke cleared at my employer's saloon. A good man."

"A *good* man?"

Haresh nodded.

Slocum drank some more coffee. "So that means whoever had told the story about that shooting was either a friend of Rob's, a family member, or a partner."

"Considering all of the detail I heard, I would gamble on partner. I hear rumors every night. They fill the air in saloons like Jocelyn's worse than cigar smoke and bad music. Most are just stories bloated with colorful language and so-called facts that are too exaggerated to be real. What I heard was exaggerated, but too close to the truth for my liking."

"So whoever spread those rumors knew what he was talking about," Slocum pointed out.

"Most likely, he was there."

"And he was a friend, relative, or partner of Rob Bensonn."

Haresh nodded. "If Abernathy himself is not here, one of his men probably is."

"Could be both. And they've been out talking to every bartender in town."

"Probably," Haresh said, "trying to track you in much the same way we are tracking them."

Slocum spotted the blond woman sauntering from the kitchen carrying a plate piled high with the food he'd ordered. He tucked a napkin into the front of his shirt and leaned back so the plate could be set in front of him. The waitress yanked her hands back and moved away after serving him as if she was dropping a hunk of raw meat in front of a hungry tiger.

Unafraid of any tiger, Haresh reached out and plucked a piece of bacon from Slocum's plate.

"That's a real good way to lose that hand," Slocum warned.

"Prove you discovered more than I did last night and I will put it back."

"Eh, keep it."

Haresh grinned victoriously while eating the bacon.

"I gotta hand it to you," Slocum said. "You went a hell of a lot further in one night than I did."

"Sounds to me like you enjoyed yourself more."

Slocum shrugged that off. "I may not have gotten the results you did, but I've got some mighty big lines in the water. Between the two of us, we should be able to find Abernathy and the rest of his men sooner rather than later."

"I agree."

"Now tell me one more thing." Slocum cut into his eggs. "Is Haresh your first name or last name?"

17

Even in the starkest rays of morning light, Chinatown seemed untouched by the sun. The garishly painted district of the flea-bitten little town retreated beneath its awnings and drawn blinds as if the residents were afraid of being exposed. That wasn't necessarily true for the actual Chinese folks living there. They went about their business just like all the rest. But like the whites, browns, or any other color in between, they had their bad seeds. For the moment, those seeds were planted deep within the drug emporiums and gambling dens of Hollister's underbelly.

The man who approached the Cat's Eye walked tall and carried himself like a true showman. Ferril Abernathy was uncomfortable handling himself any other way. He waved to the guard on his way in, daring the man to try and take his guns from him with a stern, menacing glare. The guard wasn't about to test his luck.

Once inside, he strode past the unattended front counter and went down the hall, where just under half of the doors were shut to respect customers' privacy. He knocked at Lester's office door, but didn't wait for a reply before testing the knob.

It was locked.

"Open up, Baynes," Abernathy said.

It took a while, but the chemist eventually opened the door. "Your delivery isn't ready yet."

"How far along are you?"

"Putting the finishing touches on some of it right now."

"Mind if I wait here while you complete it?"

Baynes snapped his eyes back and forth as if trying to look in every direction at once. "You wanna wait here? Why not just go somewhere and I'll send for you?"

"Because there isn't a lot of time. Certain people have been asking around about me. Considering the operation you have running here, I assumed you would have ways of ensconcing yourself so as to avoid . . ." Seeing the confused expression on his face, Abernathy clarified by saying, "I figured you'd be used to digging in so it would be safer here."

"Safe from who?"

Abernathy's eyes narrowed as he said, "You know damn well who. The lawmen that have been poking around looking for me."

Baynes shook his head and turned away from the door so he could step back into his office. "Considering how you announce yourself everywhere you go, it's a wonder you haven't been caught a dozen times already."

"My displays are carefully timed and directed at specific audiences. I assure you, when necessary I can be very discreet."

Lester's office was the same as ever, but a slender door near the back of the room had been opened. When it was closed, the door probably looked like nothing more than a loose panel in the wall easily obscured in the shadows. Although Abernathy couldn't see much of that previously hidden room, dim light from lanterns hanging on the wall reflected on curved glass of bottles and mixing bowls. More light came from within the other room in the form of flickering flames beneath beakers and metal plates. "You're as discreet as a damn peacock," Baynes muttered.

"The fact remains that someone pointed those lawmen in my direction. Someone who knew I'd be here tomorrow night to pick up a package."

"They know you're coming here?" Baynes asked.

Abernathy nodded. "Do you want to keep me hidden now?"

"Aw, Jesus! How did this happen?" The stench of burning chemicals drifted through the air, mingling with the sound of glass containers knocking against each other as Baynes hurried about his task.

"I thought we were friends, Lester. Would you rather I take my chances on the outside when I could just sit here?"

"I got a real nice business running here. Why the hell would I want to tear it apart by letting any of these half-assed lawmen or crazed vigilantes know I peddle more than pussy and opium?" Still shaking his head, Baynes grunted, "See, that was always your problem, Ferril. You never thought anything all the way through. That's why you're foolish enough to risk yer damn neck doing all those insane stunts with a gun!"

"I am *not* stupid."

"Never said you were stupid," Baynes replied while stirring a vial of murky brown liquid. "I said you're foolish. There's a difference. A man who likes to use as many fancy words as you should know as much."

"Here's a word for you. Traitor. How do you like that one?"

"I didn't tell anyone about you or our deal!" Baynes said. By now, he was fuming more than the chemicals he was mixing. "You may be a fool, but you're an old friend. Also, you're paying me damn good money to mix these chemicals so why on earth would I sell you out before I get paid?"

"Well, someone did."

After taking a beaker away from its flame, Baynes reached over to a small table to retrieve a leather case similar to the ones doctors used to hold their surgical blades. "Here's part of your order. It's the stuff that will put men to sleep. That was the easy part. There's also a bit of something that will make men loopy as hell in the little bottle with the dark stopper. Take it and go."

"Go where?"

"Away from me so I can work. If you've got lawmen or anyone else hot on your heels, I don't want them catching up to you at my place. The rest of your order will be ready when I told you it would be ready and not a moment sooner."

Abernathy took the leather case and tucked it into a pocket. "Is there a door I can use other than the one in front?"

"Step out of my office and turn right. The wall is hinged. Push it open and you'll be at the back of the building. Now . . ." He paused in the middle of his sentence and snapped his face toward the office door like a rabbit with its ears perked up.

Gruff voices came from the front portion of the opium den, followed by a woman's scream and the rumble of something heavy being overturned.

"Sounds like those lawmen you were so worried about found you," Baynes said.

Abernathy was already on his guard. "How can you be certain they're lawmen? The only other vigilantes that were close to finding me were killed back in Spencer Flats."

"Because you're the only other one to take such pains to announce yourself when you make an entrance. Best get out of here before they find their way back here."

"Are you sure about that?"

"You think I *want* them to find you here . . . with me?" Gesturing toward the elaborate setup in the hidden room, Baynes added, *"Now?"*

"Good point."

As he left the office, Abernathy distinctly heard Baynes grunt, "Idiot," before shutting the secret door to his workshop.

Abernathy stepped into the hallway and did his best to keep from walking on any loose boards as he felt around for the hinged section of wall Baynes had referred him to. His fingers found nothing but unyielding panels. The thought crossed his mind that he'd been set up for a catastrophic fall. Then again, he reasoned, Baynes wouldn't have been working so hard if he expected his client to be shot dead in a matter of minutes. As if to strengthen his faith in his old friend, the next panel Abernathy tested swung outward on well-oiled hinges.

He stepped outside, breathing a sigh of relief. Before that breath had been fully pushed from his lungs, a pair of large, brutish men stomped toward him.

"There he is!" one of them shouted while pointing at Abernathy with one hand. His other hand was already wrapped around a .45, which he brought up to fire as his partner did the same. Before either man could take their shot, a rifle cracked from higher ground, delivering a bullet to the fellow who'd done the shouting. Hot lead punched a hole through the man's chest, dropping him to the ground quicker than a kick from a mule.

"Damn it," Abernathy growled. Reflexively, he drew one of his .44s.

The surviving gunman ducked around the corner of the building and hollered, "He's out here! The bastard just killed Danny!"

More steps pounded through the front door of the Cat's Eye, leaving Abernathy with precious little time to save his skin. Outside, an armed man waited in front of a fan-tan parlor, where he could keep watch on the front portion of the Cat's Eye. Abernathy ran in that direction while firing a few quick shots, both of which chewed into the wood of the gambling parlor, causing the armed man to hop to one side before he was hit. Abernathy fired another round, but didn't draw any blood. Charging toward the fan-tan parlor, Abernathy surprised him by ignoring the gun in the other man's hand and thumping a fist into his gut.

The poke to the stomach caught the man's attention, but didn't do much else. "Who are you?" Abernathy asked.

"We're the law around here, you son of a bitch."

"I don't see a badge."

"We don't need any badges. We're the real law and we—" The second fist to pound into his stomach was wrapped around a .44, so it did considerably more than the first. The man doubled over, grunted in pain, but straightened up again.

More men charged around the building but Abernathy had no intention of meeting them. He holstered his .44, grabbed the man by the shirt, and tossed him toward the street before running in the opposite direction to seek cover within the crowd in front of the fan-tan parlor. Seconds after setting his sights on a side street that would allow him to put the vigilantes behind him, Abernathy heard more shots crack from up high. Recognizing the rifle's voice, he looked toward the rooftop of an adjacent building and shouted, "No!"

But it was too late. The shot had been fired and had found its mark. The man Abernathy had tossed in his wake swayed on trembling knees before dropping and falling face first to the ground. The hole that had been freshly blasted through his skull leaked blood and other fluids into the dirt as the men who'd forced their way into the Cat's Eye rushed outside.

"Mark!" one of them shouted. "Jesus Christ! Mark's dead!" Although more words were said, they were lost amid the thunder of wild gunfire.

Even though Abernathy was running away at the time, he could tell the vigilantes were doing all the firing by the chaotic way they pulled their triggers. Having made it across the street, he looked up to the rooftop where he knew Justin was stationed. The Winchester spat another bullet toward the opium den to knock another vigilante off his feet. That round was quickly followed by another. After that, the street was silent apart from the hushed, frightened voices of locals who'd been caught in the crossfire.

Abernathy clenched his teeth and holstered his pistol. Part of him wanted to hear more hollering behind him, just so he could know his partner hadn't finished his grisly task. But even if there were some vigilantes left alive, that wouldn't make things any better. Unfortunately, Abernathy couldn't think of a way for them to get any worse.

As with any shooting, people in the vicinity were frightened at first. Then they were curious. Abernathy spotted several folks gaping wide-eyed at the Cat's Eye as they waited for another explosion of violence. When it became apparent that the show was over, they moved in like a swarm.

Justin could no longer be seen, but that didn't matter. Abernathy had observed the rifleman at work so many times that his habits were like clockwork to him. Taking advantage of the growing confusion in the street, Abernathy skirted the crowd of people and went to the building next to the one from which Justin had been firing. He arrived less than a second after Justin had climbed down the stairs leading to that building's second floor.

"Just what in the hell do you think you're doing?" Abernathy demanded.

"Covering your ass, just like always."

"I had things well in hand!"

"Is that why them vigilantes came storming into that opium den after you?" Justin asked.

"You could have warned me about them."

"Wasn't time."

"Well then," Abernathy growled. "Seems like you've got an answer for just about everything."

"Did you get what you were after?"

"Some if it."

"Then we can come back later for the rest." Flinching toward the sound of movement nearby, Justin watched a few men race toward the Cat's Eye. "I don't know if anyone saw me up there. We'd best skin out."

"You're right. I say we split up and meet half a mile southwest of town."

"Shouldn't we stick together? What if someone else catches you? They may be watching this part of town like a bunch of hawks."

"I can slip in and out without being noticed," Abernathy assured him.

"Like you did this time?" Justin scoffed. "We should stay together."

Abernathy was on him before he could do a thing to stop it. He may have been older, but his hands were plenty strong enough to grab Justin by the collar and shake him like a rag doll when he said, "You've done quite enough here! Between you and Rob, I'd swear you men were out to kill every law-man that crosses your path! Is that it? Did someone hire you to cut through the lawmen in Montana?"

"You're talking crazy, Ferril. Besides, there ain't no real lawmen around here!"

After studying him for a few more seconds, Abernathy reluctantly let Justin go. "People will be looking away from the bodies right about now, which means we need to get moving. We're splitting up. I'm still the one calling the shots on this job, so what I say goes!"

"Naturally."

"We'll meet where I said before. After that, you stay out of sight and I'll come back for the rest of our supplies." Lowering his voice to something short of a growl, he added, "You're damn lucky we're not in California already. Folks expect things to be wild out here, but once we leave this godforsaken territory, we'll need to watch everything we say and do. That gold is still out there and we can still take it. If you want to be some kind of wild dog killer, we can part ways now and you can kill all the men you want."

Justin's lips peeled back into a filthy smile. "It's all about the gold, Ferril. You know that. We come too far to let it go now."

The people on the street may have been confused after the shooting, but they were regrouping now and starting to poke around. If there were a few sorry excuses for lawmen in town, they would be showing up soon. Any men who fancied themselves to be vigilantes would also be arriving with guns drawn, looking for something to kill.

"If you're still serious about the California job, then do as I say," Abernathy told his partner. "Ride out to our camp and lay low. I'll come back later to fetch the rest of the supplies from my acquaintance here in town. Without those chemicals, we might as well wave farewell to that California gold."

"You're the one running this outfit," Justin said.

It took every bit of showmanship at Abernathy's disposal for him to look as if he truly believed that anymore.

18

Slocum heard the shooting on his way back to The Starlight House. Haresh had an appointment to keep at a different saloon, so it hadn't been difficult to convince him to split apart after breakfast. Following the commotion to its source brought Slocum to the Chinese district. The street was filled with people milling about, trying to get a look at one of the bodies sprawled in the dirt like so many discarded toys.

"What happened here?" Slocum asked a man who stood at the periphery of one of the largest groups.

"Bob Danfield and some of his men got gunned down," he said warily.

"Was it a dispute of some kind?"

The man turned to look at Slocum as if he'd just been asked what color the sky was. He looked to be somewhere in his early to mid-fifties with a clean-shaven face that was etched with enough creases to reflect the experience he'd gained in his time on this earth. Those creases, along with the leathery condition of his skin and the hard edge to his features, made it fairly obvious he'd spent more than his share of time fending for himself in the mountains or some other equally rugged terrain. "You ain't from around here, are you?"

"No sir."

"Bob and his boys are peacekeepers."

"Lawmen?" Slocum asked.

"Closest thing we get around here," the man replied.

Vigilantes. Judging by the respect in the other man's tone, he wouldn't take kindly if the fallen peacekeepers were referred to as anything less than heroes. "Did they get the men who did this?"

"Don't know. Just got here myself."

Since Slocum was only interested in a few possible culprits, he decided to keep maneuvering through the crowds until he found a familiar face. Oddly enough, the first man he recognized wasn't among the wounded. After circling around a narrow building, he saw Haresh come around from the opposite side to meet him in the middle.

"I heard shooting," Haresh said. "Did you see what happened?"

"No, but I was told the dead men were vigilantes."

Haresh chuckled under his breath. "I was told they guarded this town, but I arrived at your same conclusion."

"And since the man I spoke to called them keepers of the peace, another conclusion we can make is that this town holds their vigilantes in high regard. That's not uncommon."

"I did not hear anyone mention Abernathy."

"Me neither," Slocum said. "But I wasn't specifically asking about him. I figure if it was him, folks would have known."

"And they would have been talking about the show he put on," Haresh added. "He is very peculiar for a gunman."

"Yes, indeed." Slocum looked around and didn't see anything other than the locals cleaning up the mess that had been left behind.

"According to the old timer I saw around front, all of these peacekeepers were chasing one man."

Since the locals were starting to take notice of them, Haresh motioned for Slocum to follow him as he walked away from the building at the center of the slaughter. "I only spoke to a few people briefly before I found you and they were all watching from afar. I doubt anyone staring at dead bodies is the sort to be up close to the ones doing the shooting. Vultures," he spat while glancing back at the onlookers. "Every last one of them."

"Even vultures have eyes. Why don't you have a word with them?" Slocum said. "Find out what you can."

"And what will you be doing?" Haresh asked.

"Pretty much the same thing but from a different angle. If Abernathy was behind this, it could be that he got what he came for and blasted his way out."

"Then shouldn't we be trying to track him down again before he gets too far from town?"

"We don't even know for certain if he is leaving town. Let's do a little more poking around before we charge out of here. I have a feeling there's more to learn."

Haresh planted his feet and gazed back at the gruesome spectacle, which was now just far enough away to observe without it sweeping him up. "Perhaps we should start here. All of the dead men are scattered around this building."

"Yeah," Slocum said while squinting in that direction. "I didn't get a good look at what that place is. Looks like a saloon or—"

"It's an opium den," Haresh said distastefully.

"I doubt a man like Abernathy would spend much time in an opium den."

"Why not? He is a killer. He is a criminal. In my experience, those are the men who have many vices."

"But not opium." Uncomfortable with the glances that were being pointed at them from the nearby locals, Slocum led Haresh away. "Liquor is one thing. It can wash some memories away for a time and loosen a man up, but it doesn't stick with you for very long. Women are another vice and there's not a damn thing wrong with them. Gambling is another one a gunman might have because he's gambling with a hell of a lot more than money every time he lays a hand on his gun. But opium is something different. It clouds your head, sets you off balance, and sticks with you for too damn long."

"And liquor doesn't do those things?"

"Liquor does some of them things, but a man can push through being drunk. His blood gets flowing fast enough through his veins and he can see straight again. Once opium has a hold on you, it's got you. And once it has you, it won't let go."

"You sound like you have experience with that vice."

"Never had much of a taste for it myself, but I've seen it work on plenty of others. Men who live and die by their gun hand steer clear of the stuff, and the ones who indulge are more like wild animals."

Haresh's eyes narrowed and he walked in methodical, plodding steps. "Abernathy is something of an animal, even if only some of the stories are to be believed. I see what you're trying to tell me. The way he kills, it is not wild. If it was, we would have caught him already."

"That's right. And if he was indulging in even a little bit of opium here today, those vigilantes would have put him down before so many of their own were shot." Slocum stood on the front porch of a clothing store that was across the street and down a ways from the Cat's Eye. From there, he could watch some of the commotion along with a few others who didn't want to get any closer to it.

"If he wasn't smoking," Haresh said while taking a position beside him, "then he must have been doing something else there."

"That's what I was thinking. How about you wait a little while and then go back over there to ask some questions? First off, it would be good to know if the man was caught inside that place or just near it."

"So you think that man was Abernathy?"

Slocum rubbed his chin. "That's the big question, now isn't it? Something in my gut tells me it is. After all, we tracked him this far and then more lawmen got killed just like they were getting killed in Tarnish Mills and Spencer Flats. That seems like too much of a coincidence if you ask me."

"I agree. So I will find out if the man who shot those vigilantes was inside the opium den. Because if he was, someone inside may know more about him."

"Or," Slocum added, "they might be able to tell us if he was Abernathy. Also, if he was inside here, I'm fairly certain it wasn't to suck on an opium pipe. That means he had other business to attend to. Knowing that might just tell us where he was headed after leaving Hollister."

"Perhaps all of his business is here."

"No," Slocum said while looking around. "Today was just more of the same. More gunfire. More lawmen dead. There's no reason for Abernathy to keep going like this unless there was something else he was aiming for. There's just nothing to be gained by announcing yourself as much as Abernathy does and leaving dead men in your wake. Especially dead lawmen. Even if they are just vigilantes, that's a whole lot of hot water without much benefit."

"Unless you're a bounty hunter."

"Abernathy is no bounty hunter. If he is, he's the dumbest one around."

"No," Haresh said. "I meant there wouldn't be much to gain unless you were a bounty hunter. Surely, there must be a price on the head of a man who does so much killing. Now that people know Abernathy is more than some rumor, there has to be a reward for his capture."

"And with every lawman that winds up dead, that price will get bigger," Slocum mused. "That's no reason for him to keep killing them, though." After thinking it over for another couple of seconds, Slocum had to shake his head.

"Abernathy is up to something beyond what we already know. If he wanted to make a living by killing folks, there's a lot better ways to go about it. Hell, he could have made a fine bounty hunter if that's what he wanted. There's something else."

"Perhaps he is here for a reason," Haresh said. "Perhaps he was at all those other towns for a reason as well. That would mean there was a purpose behind him drawing so much attention to himself all those times."

"But I don't think he drew much attention here. He just happened to get cornered. Take a look for yourself," Slocum said while motioning toward the carnage. "What you're seeing is what's left after a real big rat gnaws his way out of a trap. That makes me even more sure that there was something here other than targets to be shot."

"Then he was found when he didn't mean to be found. If so, he would have even more reason to run away from here."

Slocum swatted at the air as if he was shooing a fly. "We can go round and round about this all day or we can try to get some real answers. My vote is to get some answers, and since you're following my lead, I say we both get to it."

Haresh didn't seem very happy about following anyone's lead, but the bigger man let the statement pass. "I will see what people in that opium den know about the man who did the shooting. And then I'll ask—"

"No," Slocum cut in. "You just see what you can see about that man and then I'll do the asking. That way, maybe we'll both just seem like another couple of curious fellows trying to find out what all the excitement was about."

"It is a simple task," Haresh snarled. "I think I can do it well enough."

"It's not about trust or you doing a good job. It's about laying as low as possible for as long as we can until it's time to make a move. That's the difference between doing a job like this correctly and stumbling into a trap like an idiot. And no," Slocum quickly added. "I wasn't calling you an idiot. Just try to think about the job first and your pride later."

Haresh obviously wanted to refute some of what Slocum said. When pride had been mentioned, he visibly bristled. Still, he must have found some truth in Slocum's words because he let out a breath and reluctantly nodded. "Let's meet here," he said while looking up at the place where they were standing. "Or next door. That would be better."

The place next door was a restaurant that smelled like some of the best Chinese food Slocum had come across in a while. "All right," he said. "Meet me back here in an hour so I can see what you found out and then we'll set up another meeting after that."

"If I didn't know any better, I might think you were trying to get rid of me," Haresh said. "Or at least, trying to keep me occupied while you tend to matters on your own."

"If I wanted to ditch you so badly, all I would have had to do was tell you the wrong time I was leaving Spencer Flats. Stop being so fidgety."

"My friend is getting fidgety," Slocum said to Olivia. "Do you know why that may be?"

"Sure I do," she said. "His friend John has been checking in on him using a third party. Lots of men have a sixth sense about that sort of thing. They get fidgety, and when that happens, they get suspicious and eventually . . . they get angry."

"Only if they find out the wrong thing. Speaking of finding something out, tell me what you learned about him."

They were in her office at The Starlight House. With the curtains drawn and doors shut tight, it could very well have been the middle of the night. The illusion was broken by the quiet that had settled upon the brothel the way it always did at that time of day. Places like The Starlight House tended to get noisier at night. Slocum had passed a few of the working girls on his way in. They'd been lounging in flimsy wisps of clothing, doing their best to tempt customers, but the real lookers wouldn't be on display until later.

Olivia was dressed in dark red skirts and a black corset laced together with dark purple ribbons. Her hair was pulled neatly back and held in place by a comb decorated with a row of freshwater pearls. Rings rattled against her desk as she drummed her fingers upon its surface. "There wasn't much to learn. Most of the people I asked had never heard of him, and the ones who did were saloon owners who'd just met him yesterday. With a name and a face as distinctive as Haresh's, I would think people would remember him. Since they didn't, I guess he's nobody."

"I wouldn't go that far," Slocum said. "He's just nobody I want to shoot right now. And Abernathy?"

"He's in town, all right." She stood up and walked around her desk to give Slocum a better look at the trim curves of her hips as her skirts brushed against them. "He's got business in the Chinese district."

"I already figured as much after all the shooting earlier."

"Was that him?" she asked. "I hadn't noticed. When those boys from the logging camps come in from the mountains, the whole territory tends to get noisy."

"What business does he have in the Chinese district?"

Olivia's eyes were trained on Slocum's chest. Soon, her hands were reaching out in that same direction. Her fingers slipped between the buttoned portions of his shirt to find his skin and scratch her nails playfully against it. Despite the excited chill that went through him, Slocum grabbed her wrists to keep her from going any further. "Tell me what business he had in the Chinese district," he said.

Moving in a little more brought her close enough for him to smell the scent of her hair as she lowered her head as if unbuttoning his shirt required all of her concentration. "I don't know yet," she told him while her fingertips continued to probe beneath his shirt. All it took was a few twists to free her hands from his grip, and when she did, she looked up at him with a smile. "But I will know once my friend who operates another house in that part of town pays me a visit."

"When's that?"

"Shouldn't be for a while. He told me Abernathy will be coming back around to collect something."

"Collect what?" Slocum asked, doing his best to ignore the way Olivia brushed against him. Her leg grazed along his thigh and her breasts rubbed against him just enough for him to feel their ripe softness.

"I don't know that yet," she replied. "I'll know once my friend knows and he'll know once Abernathy comes back around to collect it. He assured me it wouldn't be for another couple of hours."

"A couple of hours?"

"At least," she nodded.

"That gives us some time."

"Yes," she said while reaching down to cup his growing erection. "It most certainly does."

"How do you propose we spend that time?"

Just because she'd already taken the lead, Slocum wasn't about to let Olivia hold the reins every step of the way. In fact, he knew the one thing she liked most was a surprise. Actually, he could think of another thing she liked but there would be time for that in a little while. First, he grabbed her wrists properly and pulled them away from his chest with enough force to send a sharp, jarring snap through her upper body. Before she could question him, he grabbed her hips and pulled her forcefully to him. He planted a powerful kiss on her mouth, and within seconds, her arms were snaking around him.

Slocum let her kiss him for a while before giving her another surprise. The instant she pulled back to take a breath, he grabbed her and spun her around. "Are you expecting any visitors?" he asked.

"Would it matter?"

He answered that by pulling up her skirts and reaching between her legs. Olivia's undergarments were thin and flimsy silk, already moistened by the slick juices of her pussy. Placing one hand on her hip, he felt between her thighs so he could rub her pussy using the entire surface of his palm. She accommodated him by spreading her legs and gripping the edges of her desk.

"You should have warned me," she whispered. "If I scream, armed men will come busting in here to help me."

"That could be a problem," Slocum replied. "Because I have a feeling you'll be doing plenty of screaming." With that, he used the tips of two fingers to rub her clit in a fast, back-and-forth motion that brought a moan up from the back of her throat.

Olivia let her head droop so her hair swayed against the top of the desk. When Slocum pulled the silk aside and slipped his fingers inside her, she let out a groan that filled the office. Sure enough, a hard knock rattled the door a second or two later.

"Miss Caster," a man on the other side said. "You all right?"

"Leave me . . . alone," she grunted as Slocum continued to rub and probe her. "I'm . . . I'm . . . fine."

There were at least two men on the other side of the door. Slocum could hear them chuckling and talking to each other as they moved away.

Slocum unbuckled his pants and hiked her skirts up over her hips. Olivia's legs were long and smooth. She arched her back while lowering her body until her breasts were almost pressed against the desk. As soon as he could, Slocum guided his cock between her thighs and entered her. Once he was inside, he grabbed her hips and pounded into her.

Olivia moaned in satisfaction. She rocked back to grind against him, moaning under her breath until she couldn't hold back any longer. When he pounded into her a few more times, she shuddered and cried out as an orgasm swept through her body. Slocum eased up and then pounded into her one more time to send her completely over the edge.

Once her climax had faded, she lifted her head and turned around to face him. "Lay down," she demanded.

"Where?"

"Just do what I told you."

Slocum liked that tone in her voice, but there was no bed or even a comfortable chair for him to use. So he lowered himself onto the floor so she could immediately straddle him. Looking up at her as she lifted her skirts made him even harder. She smiled knowingly and spread her legs to give him an even better view as she lowered herself down onto him. Bending at the knees, she reached down with one hand to guide his rigid pole between the lips of her dripping wet pussy. He could feel the instant he was inside her, and when she settled down even farther, her warm embrace slid all the way down the length of his shaft.

Keeping her knees bent, Olivia balanced on the balls of her feet and supported herself by placing both hands on Slocum's chest. She stared down at him, allowing her straight black hair to fall forward as she bobbed up and down. "You like that?" she asked.

"God, yes."

"How about this?" she asked while leaning back so she could reach around and tease the base of his cock with one hand.

Slocum couldn't find the words to tell her how good that felt. Judging by the sly grin on her face, she knew the effect she was having on him all too well.

Olivia placed both hands on his chest again and rode him in earnest. She closed her eyes and rocked back and forth while her pussy glided up and down. Every so often, she would move nothing but her hips in a fast bobbing motion that nearly drove Slocum out of his mind. He reached up with both hands to cup her buttocks, savoring the feel of the taut curves against his palms. For a while, he was content to hold her bare ass in his hands as she fucked him. Then, he grabbed her tight enough to keep her in place while he pumped up into her.

Tossing her head back, she held her breath and took every inch of him. As good as it felt, Slocum was starting to get restless. His body ached for more and he simply couldn't get it while he was on his back. When he sat up, Olivia was quick to climb off him. She crawled on the floor, propping her backside in the air like a feline offering herself to her mate. Slocum lay her on her back, rose above her, and spread her legs wide. When he drove into her, they both moaned in satisfaction.

Slocum knelt between her legs, gripping her thighs while pounding into her again and again.

Olivia turned her head and slid her fingers through her hair, grunting softly every time he impaled her with his thick member.

Now that he'd fallen into a rhythm, Slocum placed his hands upon her breasts and massaged them through the corset she wore. Above the waist, her clothes were rumpled but still in place. Below the waist, she was naked and wet. Bare legs wrapped around Slocum as he plowed into her with fierce, vigorous strokes.

Before long, her pussy clenched tight and another orgasm worked its way beneath her skin. The feeling of her muscles tensing around him combined with the urgent, pleading groans Olivia made were enough to push Slocum to his limit. He pumped into her one more time before exploding inside her. He eased partly out and then drove into her harder, which caused Olivia to scrape at the floor like a wild animal.

Even after their climaxes had subsided, they remained where they were. Both too spent to move.

Someone knocked on the door.

Without hesitation, Olivia pulled herself to her feet and

tugged her skirts more or less back into place. "Just a second," she said.

Slocum climbed reluctantly to his feet. "Can't you tell them to wait?"

"Business is business."

As she walked over to the door and reached for the handle, Slocum groused, "At least let me get my damn pants up!"

"Be quick about it," she said. "But leave your gun where it is."

She opened the door and allowed a man to step inside. He looked distinguished even though his clothes were several steps down from the finery he usually wore.

"Yes," Ferril Abernathy said as he strode inside. "Leave your gun where it lies so this doesn't get any messier than it needs to be."

19

Slocum squatted on the floor, his hand hovering a few scant inches above his holstered Colt. "I know you're fast, Abernathy. Do you think you're fast enough to stop me before I can burn you down?"

Abernathy stepped into the office and calmly shut the door behind him. "Feel free to test your luck in that regard. Many before you have tried."

Olivia walked around her desk but Slocum wasn't about to take his eyes off Abernathy to see any more than that. "Selling your friends along with information now?" he snarled. "Guess you've changed a whole lot since our days back in Texas."

"Just hear him out, John," she said. "Business is business."

"So that's all this is to you?"

"You boys want a cigar?"

Abernathy seemed interested, but didn't make a move since any twitch would have to be toward Slocum.

"So," Slocum said. "Are we gonna start shooting or do I get a chance to get dressed? That is . . . unless you like the view?"

"Imagine how I feel," Abernathy replied. "A place like this, and when I step into a room, *you're* the one I find in a state of undress."

Slocum had to fight to keep from laughing at that as he stood and hiked up his pants. Normally, it was difficult to buckle a belt one-handed. Since the alternative was lowering his guard in front of a known killer, Slocum managed just fine. He finished and put his back to a wall. "Now I'm in a real bind," he said. "I can't decide which of you I want to shoot first."

"You don't mean that, John," Olivia pouted.

"The hell I don't! I knew you weren't an upstanding citizen, but I didn't figure you'd hand me over like this."

"Ease off, Mr. Slocum," Abernathy said. "I'm not here to kill you. Surely the fact that you're standing there uninjured is proof enough of that."

"Then why are you here?"

"Ah," the older man said with half a smile. "A civilized question spoken in a civilized manner."

"Don't get used to it," Slocum warned.

"Fair enough. I came here on a business matter of my own. Part of it involved paying a visit to Miss Olivia here."

"Which," Slocum growled as he shifted toward her desk, "is something Miss Olivia failed to mention."

"Ferril had a good reason to speak with you," she said. "And you've got every reason to shoot him on sight. Seems pretty clear why I didn't let you know about this meeting. Besides, just because I let you fuck me doesn't mean I owe you an explanation for everything I do."

"There's your civility," Slocum scoffed. "Let's hear what's so damned important."

"I'll tell you the same thing I told her," Abernathy said. "I have no reason to kill you."

"At least, not here in a closed room where nobody can witness it," Slocum said,

"Exactly. I have been associating myself with a few

individuals who I thought were trustworthy. That trust has been violated and so I find myself needing to take action of a different sort."

Looking once more toward Olivia, Slocum said, "I think I know just how you feel."

"Stop acting like a child and hear him out," she snapped.

The main reason he'd continued beating that dead horse was to get a reaction from a woman whose face could be set in stone when the occasion called for it. Now that his pulse had slowed a bit and his temper had cooled, Slocum realized the situation wasn't as bad as it had seemed. Even so, he didn't know quite what to make of it just yet. "You mean those two riflemen you've got shooting over your shoulder aren't behaving?"

Abernathy was taken aback by someone exposing that fact so plainly. The stunned surprise that flicked across his face helped improve Slocum's mood a bit. "That's right," Slocum added. "I know how you've been stacking the deck in your favor."

Apparently, Abernathy was the only one surprised to hear that. "What do you mean?" Olivia asked.

While anyone might be nervous about airing their dirty laundry in front of others, airing it in front of someone in Olivia's line of work had more far-reaching consequences. "Forget it," Abernathy snapped. "He's just trying to divert us from the business at hand."

"And what might that be?" Slocum asked.

"Naturally I've associated myself with similar-minded men," Abernathy continued in something fairly close to his former tone. "I thought we were all on the same page, but it seems I was wrong. You were familiar with Rob Bensonn?"

"You know damn well I was."

"Then you should also know I did him one hell of a favor before he was killed and that's not the only way I've helped him. Upon his release from jail, he confided in me that I may be in a batch of trouble where another of my associates was concerned."

Slocum felt anger rise in him like a tide. "His release from jail? Don't you mean when he was broken out?"

"I do."

"Broken out," Slocum continued, "after a good man was shot dead in the street like a dog."

"That wasn't my doing," Abernathy said sternly.

"Right. Is that why you hired those riflemen to take shots for you? Not only do you get to look like a god with a gun in your hand, but you also get to pass the blame along for anyone getting hurt when the bullets start to fly. I was there when that saloon was shot to pieces," Slocum reminded him. "I know for a fact you did some shooting of your own."

"I'll never deny what I've done. And I surely can't deny firing my pistol. I've taken lives and will answer for it when my time comes."

"But let me guess," Slocum interrupted. "You only hurt the men that truly deserved it?"

"Most definitely," Abernathy said with a grin. "Although, I will admit, the notion of who deserves what is very subjective." His face became serious in a heartbeat. "In all my years on the wrong side of the law, I've never been one to flagrantly kill men who were simply doing their chosen profession. Killing lawmen only serves to make things more difficult. You'd be amazed how little attention is paid to a sheriff who is simply wounded in a gun battle. Those rumors are never the ones to spread. Killing lawmen in mass quantities not only draws attention, but it lights a fire under the rest of the peace officers, duly appointed or otherwise."

"And yet you seem to be leaving quite the pile of bodies behind you lately."

"Indeed I do. That brings me back to what I was saying about an associate of mine who has become more trouble than he's worth. His name is Justin Griggio."

"Never heard of him," Slocum said.

"I'm not surprised. He is one of the purest forms of predator. He doesn't care about who he kills, just so long as he can continue killing. Most of the men he's buried aren't the sort to be remembered by much of anyone. He is also a crack shot with a rifle. I found him when he approached me years ago at one of my final shows with the circus to try and make a name for himself as a trick shot artist. I thought it might be civil of me to provide a replacement performer so as not to put my show in a lurch. It didn't take much for him to display a cruel, wicked temper, and I thought it best not to expose my circus friends to such a man."

"How noble."

While there was no mistaking the sarcasm in Slocum's words, Abernathy didn't respond to it. Since Slocum's hand hadn't drifted any closer to his Colt, he resumed talking. "I've noticed you following me through the last few towns," he said. "You've proven your worth in a fight and so I decided to come to you with a proposition."

Slocum laughed. "Following you? Tracking is more like it. I was just about to cinch in around your neck like a noose. And so you decide to face me as if it was your idea. That strikes me more like a man who quits his job because he knows he's about to get fired."

"Call it what you will, Mr. Slocum. The fact remains that we are here at this moment discussing a plan that can benefit us both."

"And what might that be?"

"I hand over the man who truly killed those lawmen and in return—"

Slocum cut him short by saying, "I'm looking at the son of a bitch who killed those lawmen right now."

"If you'd been there when I approached the sheriff in Tarnish Mills, you would have seen that I tried to reason with him."

"I'll bet you did. And you kept reasoning with him until

he stepped out of line, told you to go to hell, or went for his gun while trying to do the job he gets paid to do."

Olivia had been fairly quiet until now, when she stood up and reached out for Slocum as if that would be enough to pacify him. "John, hear him out."

"You shut your goddamn mouth," Slocum barked. "You never were an angel, but I didn't think you'd stab me in the back."

"I didn't stab anyone in the back," she replied. "The deal was for Ferril to have this talk with you, and if he tried to hurt you or me, he wouldn't leave this room alive."

Slocum wasn't about to back off. "How kind of you," he sneered. "If I'd known you were on a first-name basis with this murderer, I wouldn't have bothered approaching you at all."

"I knew him back when I was about to leave Texas. Ferril helped me pull up stakes and—"

"I don't give a shit what he did," Slocum said as he shifted his full attention back to Abernathy. "What I do know is that giving the order to kill someone is just as bad as pulling the trigger. In fact, it's worse because he's too cowardly to do the deed himself."

To this point, Abernathy had been cool and composed. Although the shift in his features was barely visible, the subtle change left him looking less like a man and more like something that had been forged from iron. He stepped forward, not seeming to care that Slocum came up to meet him or that Olivia had rushed from around her desk in an attempt to get between the two men.

"I won't have this," she said.

"Well, it's what you've got, lady," Slocum told her. "Step aside and reap what you sow."

"If you'd wanted me dead so badly, you could have drawn that Colt and put it to work," Abernathy said. "The fact that you haven't tells me you're more than a simple gunman."

Slocum's reply was spoken in a voice that was

sharp enough to cut through stone. "I can kill you anytime I want."

"And I, you."

"Nobody's killing anyone," Olivia said. Since that didn't get much of a response, she added, "If a single shot is fired in here, my men will storm this room and neither one of you will walk out."

Still ignoring her, Abernathy said, "I didn't order anyone to kill those lawmen, Slocum. That's why I decided to step forward and have this talk with you right now when I could have just as easily lured you somewhere suitable for either myself or my partner to pick you off."

"All right, then," Slocum said. "What do you want from me that's so damned important?"

Abernathy took a deep breath and let it out. "I want you to clear my good name."

"Even if half of the stories about you are to be believed," Slocum said, "your name isn't all that good."

"I know what is attached to my name, sir. I'm the one who made it what it is. I am a legend with these guns," Abernathy stated as he patted the .44s at his side. "I am a man to be feared. I am a thief. No . . . make that a spectacular thief. I am the one who put on displays of skill that will be in the minds of the legions of people who came to see me in my circus days. And yes. I am a killer. But I am *not* a man who put a man in his grave without good reason. And I am no coward."

No matter how badly Slocum wanted to refute that statement, he had to give the other man some credit for making his appearance and keeping his composure for this long. "I suppose I can give you that last part." Finishing buckling his pants, he admitted, "This isn't the first time I've been caught off my guard. Most of the time, a man in your position would either knock me out or disarm me before speaking their piece. That either makes you overconfident or stupid. But I guess neither one of them is a coward."

Abernathy nodded solemnly.

"Whatever you've done," Slocum continued, "you've made your bed and you'll lie in it. What do you want me to do when it comes to clearing your name?"

"You can spread the word. I've heard of you, John Slocum. You've earned some measure of respect among lawmen. I want you to set the records straight where these dead lawmen are concerned. Tell whoever you can, whenever the opportunity presents itself, that Ferril Abernathy made a stupid mistake but he didn't gun down those lawmen in cold blood. And yes, Olivia," he added reluctantly as if the gravity of his words was just now sinking in, "that means you spreading the truth through your various channels as well. In exchange for that simple courtesy, I will hand over the man responsible for the deaths of those lawmen, the vigilantes that were killed here, and several others. You can do with him as you please. Since you tracked me down this far, I assume justice is what you were after. Possibly also a reward for bringing down the killer of that sheriff from Tarnish Mills. When you get Justin Griggio, you'll have those things."

"And then what?" Slocum asked.

"Then we part ways. Our business will be concluded. If you want to take the matter any further, you can have your chance for that as well by challenging me whenever you see fit. If you'd prefer, we can wrap things up here and then part ways. What do you say, Mr. Slocum? Interested in this deal?"

"Why should I believe we'll just part ways?"

"You've got your gun right now," Abernathy said. "You'll have it every step of the way. If you ever want to change the deal or put me to the test, you'll have your chance. All I ask right now is that you help me take down the one man who truly deserves your wrath."

Slocum studied him for a second before saying, "All right, then. But first, I want to go to that shop in Chinatown so you can show me what the hell you were after there. I don't want to just hear it from you," he added before Abernathy could protest. "I want you to show me. After that, do whatever you can to make sure that partner of yours comes along with me back to Tarnish Mills. If that means talking sense into him, distracting him so I can get a clear shot, or even lying to him to make him drop his guard, then so be it."

"But—"

"No buts," Slocum cut in. "You want me to put some faith in you, then you can do the same right now with me. If nothing else, it'll be a gesture to let me know you're worthy of any good words I might spread about you from this point on."

Without a word, Abernathy nodded and motioned for Slocum to precede him on his way out of the room. It wasn't much of a surprise when Slocum refused that offer and Abernathy calmly put his back to the room and stepped outside.

As Slocum moved in to follow, Olivia came along as well. "John," she said. "Let me explain."

"No," he said in a clipped tone. "I don't want to hear one more goddamn word from you."

She fell silent and let both of them go on without her.

20

Slocum's plan was simple. He meant to take Abernathy to the Cat's Eye in the Chinese district and hope Haresh was still in the vicinity, ready to back him up. He didn't know where Abernathy's rifleman partner was, which meant he could be anywhere. And since he could be anywhere at any given time, he was practically not a factor. It never did anyone a lick of good to try and plan around a wild card. Slocum would play to whatever advantages he had, rely on his skill, and hope for the best. There would be some luck involved, but he was used to that.

As soon as they got within sight of the Cat's Eye, Abernathy became suspicious. "How did you know I have business in this part of town?"

Slocum stopped and turned to face him. He was practically in the middle of the street, so if Haresh was in the area, he would have to see him. "Olivia told me. What do you think?"

"If you are trying to lure me somewhere, I wouldn't advise it. Justin may not be the sharpest knife in the drawer, but he's survived by being able to—" Abernathy was cut short when a shot erupted from Slocum's left to send a bullet whipping through the air between the two men.

Slocum drew his Colt and rushed for cover. He wound up behind a post that supported the awning of a store advertising exotic spices from the mysterious Orient. "Your boy's lost his touch, Abernathy!" he shouted.

But the older man was seeking cover as well. Another shot blasted through the air, shattering a window behind him. "That's not Justin!" Abernathy hollered. "Whoever it is, he's shooting at *me*, damn it!"

Sure enough, when Slocum peeked around the post, he saw more glass shattering in a window behind the spot where Abernathy had dived behind a water trough. Another shooter cut loose, and when Slocum traced the shots to their source, he found Haresh standing in front of a tea shop. The bigger man had shifted his aim toward Justin, who stood at the mouth of an alley about seventy yards from Slocum and Abernathy. The large man was a piss-poor shot, but at least he'd forced the first rifleman to cease fire for the moment.

"Keep me covered, Haresh!" Slocum shouted.

The big man nodded once and then was spun around by a shot that clipped him in the shoulder.

The buildings in the Chinese district closed in to create narrow streets that twisted at odd angles. Justin pressed himself against one of the buildings that formed the alley. "That was a warning," he shouted. "And it's the only one you're gonna get!"

"Justin!" Abernathy bellowed. "Get away from here before this gets any worse!"

"It's already as worse as it's gonna get! It's over, Ferril! It's been over since you got that crazy idea to do that cockamamie scheme of yours."

"So you get us all killed here? That's your solution?"

"It was gonna happen sooner or later," Justin replied as people ran back and forth in front of him to try and clear a path for the gunfire. "You may not get all that gold you keep going on about, but that won't stop me from gettin' rich! Thanks to all the lawmen you gunned down, you got a price on your head big enough to set me up for the rest of my life!"

"I won't allow you to walk away after double-crossing me," Abernathy warned.

Without hesitating, Justin sighted along the top of his rifle and fired a shot that caught Abernathy in the chest. "You ain't got anything more to say about it," he said while the older man dropped.

By now, Slocum had inched toward Abernathy's blind side while Haresh crossed the street to make his way toward the alley. Justin was about to say something else when he caught sight of Haresh and snapped his rifle toward him for a quick shot. Rather than dive for cover, Haresh let out a wild scream and charged at him while firing every last bullet from his cylinder.

Justin was so rattled by the sight of Haresh coming at him like a crazed rhino that the single shot he squeezed off sailed well above the row of storefronts in front of him. Having emptied his gun, Haresh tossed the weapon and pulled a knife from a scabbard that hung at his side. On his hip, the knife looked like one carried by just about anyone for hunting or anything else. Now that it was drawn, the blade looked more like a machete. Only a man as big as Haresh could have swung it without breaking stride.

Still rattled by the sight of the big man, Justin didn't attempt anything fancy. He barely had enough time before Haresh got to him. Aiming low, he took a shot that a blind man could have made. His bullet carved a path through Haresh's leg, and when the bigger man took his next step, he dropped to one knee and let out a pained groan. Justin drew his pistol and rushed over to wrap one arm around Haresh's neck. Holding him up like a shield, he pointed the gun at his head and roared, "Toss that pistol, Slocum! This never was yer fight to start with!"

"I made it mine," Slocum replied. "And I aim to finish it."

"Yeah? Do that and this savage dies first."

"Savage?" Haresh roared.

Justin pounded his foot against the fresh wound in the big man's leg. "Shut yer hole, savage!"

Slocum studied the angles and didn't like what he found. Haresh was so large that Justin had more cover than if he'd ducked behind damn near anything else in the vicinity apart from one of the buildings. Slocum's only targets were a sliver of one of Justin's arms and less than a quarter of his head as he peeked around his human shield. Considering the distance between him and his target, Slocum figured his odds of hitting Justin without spilling Haresh's blood stood at no better than ten percent.

Those odds were halved when Justin nervously tucked himself a bit farther behind Haresh.

"We're not the only men that will be coming after you," Slocum said. "Now that you've tipped your hand, every lawman and vigilante for miles around will be on your trail. Let that man go before this gets any worse."

"Ain't no more to bargain with," Justin replied. "Me and this savage here are leaving town. Anyone follows me and they'll die a few seconds after this one here. I earned my keep putting men down from a distance. I ain't worried about getting away from—"

A single shot cracked through the air.

Justin's head snapped back and his arm fell limp to his side, allowing the pistol to slide from his grasp.

Haresh was left standing by himself. After taking a moment to catch his breath, he bent down and picked up the other man's gun.

From what Slocum could see, that single shot had traveled along Justin's arm like a rock skimming across the top of still water, tearing the limb up badly enough to keep him from maintaining a grip on his weapon. From there, it punched through Justin's neck and exploded out the back of his head.

"Thank you, John," Haresh said.

"Wasn't me." Turning around, Slocum found the man who'd fired that shot. Even more impressive, Abernathy had done it while lying on his side and bleeding from the wound that he'd gotten at the start of the commotion.

Slocum walked over to Abernathy. The older man was pale and no longer had the strength to lift his .44. "Didn't . . . mean for this . . . to get so bloody," Abernathy said.

Kneeling down to him, Slocum said, "It's over now."

"You . . . must think I'm a . . . terrible person."

"Doesn't matter what I think anymore."

"No. S-Suppose not. Is your friend hurt?"

"Doesn't look like it."

Abernathy managed half of one nod. "This . . . got out of hand. That's all."

"Yeah. It sure did."

Abernathy's eyes glazed over and fixed upon a point well beyond Slocum. "Damn. I never . . . never got to . . . California."

The old man's body went limp and people began closing in around the gruesome spectacle. Haresh shoved his way through to arrive at Slocum's side carrying Justin's rifle.

"That other one's dead?" Slocum asked.

"Most definitely." Looking down at Abernathy as if the old man were still in the circus, Haresh asked, "Was he talking to you?"

"Yeah. Something about wanting to go to California."

"What for?"

Slocum shrugged and stood up. "Hell if I know."

"So what were they looking for here in town?"

"Don't know."

Now Haresh looked over at Slocum as if he were the display. "Don't you care to know these things?"

"The job I took was to track down the men who killed Sheriff Cass and the rest of those lawmen to make certain they paid for their crimes. No man can pay more than what these two did here today."

"That one back there said he was out to collect a reward for his partner's capture."

More people were coming out of the woodwork, gaping at the bloody spectacle of the two dead men. Slocum sighed. "Near as I can tell, the one with the rifle shot the lawmen while Abernathy stood up front trying to further his own ends. As to what those ends were, I couldn't tell you. I've seen plenty of men die, and every last one had a world of history behind them. More often than not, they don't answer for every last sin they committed and rarely finish every task they started. When their time comes, it's all over. The reaper don't give a damn how many irons you had in the fire."

Slocum and Haresh stood there, looking down at Abernathy as if they could read one last page of the old man's story by staring at him long enough.

They would have to settle for the legends Abernathy left behind.

As for Justin, the only one interested in him was the undertaker, who'd scurried out of his shop to take his measurements.

DON'T MISS A YEAR OF

Slocum Giant
by
Jake Logan

penguin.com/actionwesterns

M457AS0510

GIANT-SIZED ADVENTURE FROM AVENGING ANGEL LONGARM.

BY TABOR EVANS

penguin.com/actionwesterns

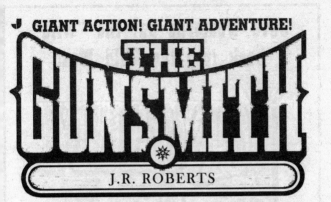

GIANT ACTION! GIANT ADVENTURE!

THE GUNSMITH

J.R. ROBERTS

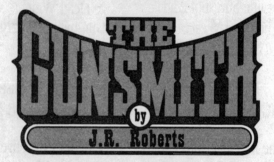